I0542273

An
Amiable Charlatan

E. Phillips Oppenheim

1st WORLD
LIBRARY
Literary Society

An Amiable Charlatan

E. Phillips Oppenheim

© 1st World Library – Literary Society, 2004
PO Box 2211
Fairfield, IA 52556
www.1stworldlibrary.org
First Edition

LCCN: 2004195287

Softcover ISBN: 1-4218-0114-0
Hardcover ISBN: 1-4218-0014-4
eBook ISBN: 1-4218-0214-7

Purchase *"An Amiable Charlatan"*
as a traditional bound book at:
www.1stWorldLibrary.org/purchase.asp?ISBN=1-4218-0114-0

1st World Library Literary Society is a nonprofit organization dedicated to promoting literacy by:

- Creating a free internet library accessible from any computer worldwide.
- Hosting writing competitions and offering book publishing scholarships.

Readers interested in supporting literacy through sponsorship, donations or membership please contact:
literacy@1stworldlibrary.org
Check us out at: www.1stworldlibrary.ORG
and start downloading free ebooks today.

An Amiable Charlatan
contributed by Tim, Ed & Rodney
in support of
1st World Library Literary Society

CONTENTS

CHAPTER I

THE MAN AT STEPHANO's

The thing happened so suddenly that I really had very little time to make up my mind what course to adopt under somewhat singular circumstances. I was seated at my favorite table against the wall on the right-hand side in Stephano's restaurant, with a newspaper propped up before me, a glass of hock by my side, and a portion of the *plat du jour*, which happened to be chicken *en casserole*, on the plate in front of me.

I was, in fact, halfway through dinner when, without a word of warning, a man who seemed to enter with a lightfooted speed that, considering his size, was almost incredible, drew a chair toward him and took the vacant place at my table. My glass of wine and my plate were moved with smooth and marvelous haste to his vicinity. Under cover of the tablecloth a packet - I could not tell what it contained - was thrust into my hand.

"Sir," he said, raising my glass of wine to his lips, "I am forced to take somewhat of a liberty. You can render me the service of a lifetime! Kindly accept the situation."

I stared at him for a moment quite blankly. Then I

recognized him; and, transferring at once the packet to my trousers pocket, I drew another glass toward me and poured out the remainder of my half-bottle of hock. So much, at any rate, I felt I had saved!

"I shall offer you presently," my self-invited guest continued, with his mouth full of my chicken, "the fullest explanation. I shall also ask you to do me the honor of dining with me. I think I am right in saying that we are not altogether strangers?"

"I know you very well by sight," I told him. "I have seen you here several times before with a young lady."

"Exactly," he agreed. "My daughter, sir."

"Then for the sake of your daughter," I said, with an enthusiasm that was not in the least assumed, "I can assure you that, whether as host or guest, you are very welcome to sit at my table. As for this packet - "

"Keep it for a few moments, my young friend," the newcomer interrupted, "just while I recover my breath, that is all. Have confidence in me. Things may happen here very shortly. Sit tight and you will never regret it. My name, so far as you are concerned, is Joseph H. Parker. Tell me, you are facing the door, some one has just entered. Who is it?"

"A stranger," I replied; "a stranger to this place, I am sure. He is tall and dark; he is a little lantern-jawed - a hatchet-shaped face, I should call it."

"My man, right enough," Mr. Joseph H. Parker muttered. "Don't seem to notice him particularly," he added, "but tell me what he is doing."

E. Phillips Oppenheim

"He seems to have entered in a hurry," I announced, "and is now taking off his overcoat. He is wearing, I perceive, a bowler hat, a dinner jacket, the wrong-shaped collar; and he appears to have forgotten to change his boots."

"That's Cullen, all right," Mr. Joseph H. Parker groaned. "You're a person of observation, sir. Well, I've been in tighter corners than this - thanks to you!"

"Who is Mr. Cullen and what does he want?" I asked.

"Mr. Cullen," my guest declared, sampling the fresh bottle of wine which had just been brought to him, "is one of those misguided individuals whose lack of faith in his fellows will bring him some time or other to a bad end. My young friend, sip that wine thoughtfully - don't hurry over it - and tell me whether my choice is not better than yours?"

"Possibly," I remarked, with a glance at the yellow seal, "your pocket is longer. By the by, your friend is coming toward us."

"It is not a question of pocket," Mr. Parker continued, disregarding my remark, "it is a question of taste and judgment; discrimination is perhaps the word I should use. Now in my younger days - Eh? What's that?"

The person named Cullen had paused at my table. His hand was resting gently upon the shoulder of my self-invited guest. Mr. Parker looked up and appeared to recognize him with much surprise.

"You, my dear fellow!" he exclaimed. "Say, I'm delighted to see you - I am sure ! But would you mind - just a little lower with your fingers! Too professional a touch altogether!"

Mr. Cullen smiled, and from that moment I took a dislike to him - a dislike that did much toward determining the point of view from which I was inclined to consider various succeeding incidents. He was by no means a person of prepossessing appearance. His cheeks were colorless save for a sort of yellowish tinge. His mouth reminded me of the mouth of a horse; his teeth were irregular and poor.

Yet there was about the man a certain sense of power. His eyes were clear and bright. His manner was imbued with the reserve strength of a man who knows his own mind and does not fear to speak it.

"I am sorry to interrupt you at your dinner, Mr. Parker," he said, his eyes traveling all over the table as though taking in its appointments and condition.

"Of no consequence at all," Mr. Parker assured him; "in fact I have nearly finished. If you are thinking of dining here let me recommend this chicken *en casserole*. I have tasted nothing so good for days!"

Mr. Cullen thanked him mechanically. His mind, however, was obviously filled with other things. He was puzzled.

"You must have a double about this evening, I fancy," he remarked. "I could have sworn I saw you coming out of a certain little house in Adam Street not a couple of minutes ago. You know the little house I mean?"

Mr. Parker smiled.

"Seems as though that double were all right," he said. "I am halfway through my dinner, as you can see, and I'm a slow eater - especially in pleasant company. Shake hands with my friend - Mr. Paul Walmsley, Mr. Cullen."

My surprise at hearing my own name correctly given was only equaled by the admiration I also felt for my companion's complete and absolute assurance. Mr. Cullen and I exchanged a perfunctory handshake, which left me without any change in my feelings toward him.

"Another of my mistakes, I suppose," Mr. Cullen said quietly. "I am afraid on this occasion, however, that I must trouble you, Mr. Parker. An affair of a few moments only. I won't even suggest Bow Street - at present. If you could take a stroll with me - even into Luigi's office would do."

Mr. Parker put down his knife and fork with a little gesture of irritation. His broad, good-natured face was for the moment clouded. "Say, Cullen," he remonstrated, "don't you think you're carrying this a bit too far, you know? There isn't a man I enjoy a half-hour's chat with more than you; but in the middle of dinner - dinner with a friend too - "

"I try to do my duty," Mr. Cullen interrupted, "and I am afraid that I am not at liberty to study your comfort."

Mr. Parker sighed heavily.

"Do you mind, Walmsley, having my plate kept warm and reminding the man that I ordered asparagus to follow?" my new friend remarked, as he rose to his feet. "Mr. Cullen wants a word or two with me in private, and Mr. Cullen is a man who will have his own way."

I nodded as indifferently as possible and the two men walked off together toward the entrance. Then I summoned my waiter.

"Bring me," I ordered, "a fresh portion of chicken and order some asparagus to follow. Keep my friend's chicken warm and order him some asparagus also."

Leaning back in my chair I tried to puzzle out the probable meaning of this somewhat extraordinary happening. My acquiescence in the attitude that had been so suddenly forced upon me was owing entirely to one circumstance. Mr. Joseph H. Parker I had recognized at his first entrance as a regular *habitué* of the restaurant. He was usually accompanied by a young lady who, from the first moment I had seen her, had produced an effect upon my not too susceptible disposition for which I was wholly unable to account, but which was the sole reason why I had given up my club and all other restaurants and occupied that particular place for the last fortnight.

I had put the two down as an American and his daughter traveling in England for pleasure; and my continual presence at the restaurant was wholly inspired by the hope that some opportunity might arise by means of which I could make their acquaintance. Adventures, in the ordinary sense of the word, had never appealed to me. I was privileged to possess many charming acquaintances among the other sex, but not one of them had ever inspired me with anything save the most ordinary feelings of friendship and admiration.

The opportunity I desired had now apparently come. I had made the acquaintance of Mr. Joseph H. Parker - made it in an unceremonious manner, perhaps, but still under circumstances that would probably result in his being willing to acknowledge himself my debtor. I had a packet of something belonging to him in my pocket, which was presumably valuable. His friend, Mr. Cullen, I detested, and the reference to Bow Street puzzled me. However, I had no doubt that in a few minutes everything would be explained. Meantime I permitted myself to indulge in certain very pleasurable anticipations.

In the course of about a quarter of an hour Mr. Joseph H. Parker reappeared. He came down the room humming a tune and apparently quite pleased with himself. I took the opportunity of studying his personal appearance a little more closely. He was not tall, but he was distinctly fat. He had a large double chin, but a certain freshness of complexion and massiveness about his forehead relieved his face from any suspicion of grossness. He had a large and humorous mouth, delightful eyes and plentiful eyebrows. His iron-gray hair was brushed carefully back from his forehead. He gave one the idea of strength, notwithstanding the disabilities of his figure. He smiled contentedly as he seated himself once more at my table.

"Really," he began, "I scarcely know how to excuse myself, Mr. Walmsley. However, thanks to you, we can now dine in comfort. Until now I fear I have taken your good offices very much for granted; but I assure you it will give me the greatest pleasure to make your closer acquaintance and to impress upon you my extreme sense of obligation."

"You are very kind," I replied. "By the by, might I ask how you know my name?"

"My young friend," Mr. Parker said, eying with approval the fresh portion of chicken that had been brought him, "it is my business to know many things. I go about the world with my eyes and ears open. Things that escape other people interest me. Your name is Mr. Paul Walmsley. You are one of a class of men that practically doesn't exist in America. You have no particular occupation that I know of, save that you have a small estate in the country, which no doubt takes up some of your time. You have rooms in London, which you occupy occasionally. You probably write a little - I have noticed that you are fond of watching people."

"You really seem to know a good deal about me," I confessed, a little taken aback.

"I am not far from the mark, am I?"

"You are not," I admitted.

"As regards your lack of occupation," Mr. Parker went on, "I am not the man to blame you for it. There are very few things in life a man can settle down to nowadays. To a person of imagination the ordinary routine of the professions and the ordinary curriculum of business life is a species of slavery. We live in overcivilized times. There seems to be very little room anywhere for a man to gratify his natural instincts for change and adventure."

I murmured my acquiescence with his sentiments and my companion paused for a few minutes, his whole attention devoted to his dinner.

"Might one inquire," I asked, after a brief pause, "as to your own profession? You are an American, are you not?"

"I am most certainly an American," Mr. Parker assented.

"In business?" I asked.

Mr. Parker looked round. Our table was comparatively isolated.

"I am an adventurer," he replied mysteriously.

I stared at him and repeated the word. He beamed pleasantly upon me.

"An adventurer! My daughter, whom you have seen here with me, is an adventuress. We live by our wits and we do pretty well at it. Sometimes we live in luxury. Sometimes we are up against it good and hard. The Ritz one day, you know, and Bloomsbury the next; but lots of fun all the time."

I looked at him a little blankly.

"To a certain extent I suppose you are joking?" I asked.

"To no extent at all," he assured me. "By the by, as regards that packet; would you mind just slipping it under this newspaper?"

I withdrew it from my pocket and obeyed him at once. Mr. Parker's fingers seemed to play with it for a moment and I noticed at that moment what a strong and capable hand he seemed to have, with fingers of unusual length and suppleness.

A dark faced *maître d'hôtel*, who presided over our portion of the room, came up smiling, with an inquiry as to our coffee. He exchanged a casual sentence or two with Mr. Parker, bowed and passed on. Mr. Parker, a moment later, with a little smile lifted the newspaper. The packet had disappeared. He noticed my look of surprise and seemed gratified.

"A mere trifle, that!" he declared. "I can assure you that I could have taken it out of your pocket, if I had desired, without your feeling a thing."

"Wonderful!" I murmured, feeling distinctly uncomfortable.

"Just a gift!" he continued modestly. "We all have our talents, you know. I have ordered some special coffee."

I was beginning to think rapidly now.

"By the by," I asked, "what is Mr. Cullen's profession?"

"He is a detective," Mr. Parker answered, without hesitation; "and, to my mind, a singularly bad one. For two months he has had what they call his eye on me. Between ourselves I think he will have his eye on me still in another two months' time. I am sure I hope so, for I frankly admit that half the savor of life would be gone if my friend, Mr. Cullen, were to finally give me up as a bad job and leave me alone."

I suppose that something of what I was feeling was reflected in my face. I had always considered myself a man of the world and I was interested enough in my fellows to enjoy mixing with all classes.

But there was the girl!

"You are thinking - !" my companion began softly.

"Your friend," I interrupted, "has just entered the restaurant. He is coming toward this table."

Mr. Parker's expression never changed. Not a muscle twitched. His tone was even careless.

"Just as well, perhaps," he remarked, "that we worked that little conjuring trick."

The detective stood once more at our table. My instinctive dislike of him was now an accomplished thing. I hated his smile of subdued triumph, and all my fundamental ideas as to law and order were seriously affected by it. I was distinctly on the side of my new acquaintance.

"I am sorry to interrupt this little feast," Mr. Cullen said, "but I shall have to trouble you both to come with me for a short time."

Mr. Parker carefully clipped the end of his cigar and leaned back in his chair while he lit it.

"My friend Cullen," he remonstrated, "I have no objection to offering myself up as a victim to your super-abundant energy and trotting about with you wherever you choose; but when it comes to dragging my friends into it, I just want to say right here that I think you are carrying things a little too far - just a little too far, sir."

"If either of you seriously object to my request," Mr. Cullen replied doggedly, "I can put the matter on a different basis."

"Who is this friend of yours and why should we go anywhere with him?" I asked.

Mr. Parker shook his head mournfully.

"You may well ask," he sighed. "You may not think it, to look at his ingenuous and honest expression, but the fact, nevertheless, remains that Mr. Cullen is a misguided but zealous member of the Sherlock Holmes fraternity: in short, a detective."

I rose to my feet with some alacrity.

"Anything in the shape of an adventure - " I began.

"Not much adventure about this," Mr. Parker interrupted gloomily, brushing the ashes from his waistcoat and also rising. "We are probably going to be searched for spoons. However if it must be - "

For the first time in my life I walked side by side with a detective. He led us to the far end of the restaurant, into an apartment usually used by the manager as a wine-tasting office, and carefully closed the door behind us. Outside I caught the glimmer of a policeman's helmet.

"Every precaution taken, you perceive," Mr. Parker remarked. "In case we should turn out to be desperate characters and, appalled by the fear of discovery, should be driven to make a personal attack upon Mr. Cullen, a myrmidon of the law is lurking near. Under those circumstances I shall eschew violence. I shall submit myself peaceably to a second examination."

I found the affair, on the whole, interesting. I divested myself only of my coat and waistcoat and Mr. Cullen's fingers did the rest. Only a single and momentary frown betrayed his disappointment as, ten minutes later, he unlocked the door.

"Gentlemen," he said, "I owe you my most profound apologies."

"That's all right, Cullen," Mr. Parker observed, patting him on the shoulder; "but let's have this thing straight now. Are we to be allowed to finish our dinner in peace or will you be turning up again with a new idea? And if I take a box for the Tivoli presently, shall we have the pleasure of seeing you bob in upon us?"

"So far as my present intentions are concerned," Mr. Cullen remarked grimly, "you may rely upon remaining undisturbed. I am sorry, Mr. Walmsley," he added, turning to me, "to have been the cause of any annoyance to you this evening. My advice to you is, if you wish to escape these inconveniences through life, to avoid the society of people whose character is known to the police."

"I shall get you for libel yet, Cullen!" Mr. Parker declared, pulling down his waistcoat.

"What I've done to annoy that man I can't imagine," he went on impersonally. "Mind, he practises on me - I'm convinced of it."

Mr. Cullen left us abruptly and quitted the restaurant. I returned to our table with my new friend.

"Really," he said, "I scarcely know how to apologize to you, Mr. Walmsley. This sort of thing amuses me, as a rule; but I must admit that Mr. Cullen is apt to get on one's nerves. A well-meaning man, mind, but unduly persistent!"

I resumed my seat at the table. I was feeling a little dazed. Opposite, talking to two ladies, was the smooth-faced *maître d'hôtel* into whose keeping I felt sure that packet had gone. Seated by my side was the gentleman who had assured me with the utmost self-possession that he was an adventurer. And standing in the doorway, looking at us, was the girl who for the last few weeks had monopolized all my thoughts; who had played havoc to such a complete extent with the principles of my life that, for her sake, I was at that moment perfectly willing to range myself even among the outcasts of the world.

E. Phillips Oppenheim

CHAPTER II

THE COUP IN THE GAMBLING DEN

On seeing us the girl advanced into the room. I called Mr. Parker's attention to her and he rose at once to his feet. It was a cold evening in April and she was wearing a long coat trimmed with some dark-colored fur, and a hat also trimmed with fur, but with something blue in it. She was rather tall; she had masses of dark brown hair, a suspicion of a fringe, and deep blue eyes. She came toward us very deliberately, with the same grace of movement I had watched and admired night after night. She gave me a glance of the slightest possible curiosity as she approached. Then her father introduced us.

"This is Mr. Paul Walmsley, my dear," he said - "my daughter. Have you dined, Eve?"

She shook hands with me and smiled very charmingly.

"Hours ago," she replied. "I didn't mean to come out this evening, but I was so bored that I thought I would try and find you."

She accepted the chair I was holding and unbuttoned her cloak.

"You will have some coffee?" I begged.

"Why, that would be delightful," she agreed. "I am so glad to find you with my father, Mr. Walmsley," she continued. "I know he hates dining alone; but this evening I had an appointment with a dressmaker quite late - and I didn't feel a bit like dinner anyhow."

"You come here often, don't you?" I ventured.

"Very often indeed," she replied. "You see it is not in the least entertaining where we are staying and the cooking is abominable. Then father adores restaurants. Do tell me what you have been talking about - you two men - all the evening?"

"The truth!" Mr. Parker remarked, lighting another cigar. "My daughter knows that I speak nothing else. It is a weakness of mine. Mr. Walmsley and I were exchanging notes as to our relative professions. I told him frankly that I was an adventurer and you an adventuress. I think by now he is beginning to believe it."

She laughed very softly - almost under her breath; yet I fancied there was a note of mockery in her mirth.

"Confess that you were very much shocked, Mr. Walmsley!" she said.

"Not in the least," I assured her.

She raised her eyebrows ever so slightly.

"Confess, then," she went on, "confess, Mr. Walmsley, that in all your well-ordered life you have never heard such an admission made by two apparently respectable people before."

"How do you know," I asked, "that my life has been well-ordered?"

"Look at yourself in the glass," she begged.

Scarcely knowing what I did, I turned round in my seat and obeyed her. There is, perhaps, a certain preciseness about my appearance as well as my attire. I am tall enough - well over six feet - but my complexion still retains traces of my years in Africa and of my fondness for outdoor sports. My hair is straight and I have never grown beard or mustache. I felt, somehow, that I represented the things which in an Englishman are a little derided by young ladies on the other side of the water.

"I can't help my appearance," I said, a little crossly. "I can assure you that I am not a prig."

"Our young friend," Mr. Parker intervened, "has certainly earned his immunity from any such title. To tell you the truth, Eve, he has already been my accomplice this evening in a certain little matter. But for his help, who knows that I might not have found myself up against it? Between us we have even had a little fun out of Cullen."

Her expression changed. She seemed, for some reason, none too well pleased.

"What have you been doing?" she asked me.

"I, personally, have been doing very little indeed," I told her. "Your father entered the restaurant in a hurry about an hour ago and found it convenient to seat himself at my table and help himself to my dinner. He intrusted me, also, with a packet, which I subsequently returned to him."

"It is now," Mr. Parker declared, replying to his daughter's anxious glance, "in perfectly safe hands."

She sighed and shook her head at him.

"Daddy," she murmured plaintively, "why will you run such risks? Even Mr. Cullen isn't an absolute idiot, you know, and there might have been some one else watching."

Mr. Parker nodded.

"You are quite right, my dear," he admitted. "To tell you the truth, Cullen was really a little smarter than usual this evening. However, there's always the luck, you know - our luck! If Mr. Walmsley had turned out a different sort of man - but, then, I knew he wouldn't."

She turned her head and looked at me. She had a trick of contracting the corners of her eyes just a little, which was absolutely bewitching.

"Will you tell me why you helped my father in this way, Mr. Walmsley?"

I returned her regard steadfastly.

"It never occurred to me," I said, "to do anything else - after I had recognized him."

She smiled a little. My speech was obviously sincere. I

think from that moment she began to realize why I had occupied the little table, opposite to the one where she so often sat, with such unfailing regularity.

"What about a music hall?" Mr. Parker suggested. "I hear there's a good show on right across the street here. Have you any engagement for this evening, Mr. Walmsley?"

"None at all," I hastened to assure him.

We left the place together a few minutes later and found a vacant box at the Tivoli. Arrived there, however, Mr. Parker soon became restless. He kept on seeing friends in the auditorium. We watched him, with his hat a little on the back of his head, going about shaking hands in various directions.

"How long have you been in England?" I asked my companion.

"Barely two months," she replied. "Do look at father! Wherever he goes it's the same. The one recreation of his life is making friends. The people he is speaking to to-night he has probably come across in a railroad train or an American bar. He makes lifelong friendships every time he drinks a cocktail, and he never forgets a face."

"Isn't that a little trying for you?" I asked.

She laughed outright.

"If you could only see some of the people he brings up and introduces to me!"

We talked for some time upon quite ordinary subjects. As the time passed on, however, and her father did not return, it seemed to me she became more silent. She told me very little about herself and the few personal things she said were always restrained. I was beginning to feel almost discouraged; she sat so long with a slight frown upon her forehead and her head turned away from me.

"Miss Parker," I ventured at last, "something seems to have displeased you."

"It has," she admitted.

"Will you please tell me what it is?" I asked humbly. "If I have said or done anything clumsy give me a chance, at any rate, to let you see how sorry I am."

She turned and faced me then.

"It is not your fault," she assured me; "only I am a little annoyed with my father."

"Why?"

"I think," she went on, "it is perfectly delightful that he should have made your acquaintance. It isn't that at all. But I do not think he should have made use of you in the way he did. He is utterly reckless sometimes and forgets what he is doing. It is all very well for himself, but he has no right to expose you to - to - "

"To what risk did he expose me?" I demanded. "Tell me, Miss Parker - was he absolutely honest when he told me he was an adventurer?"

E. Phillips Oppenheim

"Absolutely!"

"Was I, then, an accomplice in anything illegal to-night?"

"Worse than illegal - criminal!" she told me.

Now my father had been a judge and I had a brother who was a barrister; but the madness was upon me and I spoke quickly and convincingly.

"Then all I have to say about it is that I am glad!" I declared.

"Why?" she murmured, looking at me wonderingly.

"Because he is your father and I have helped him," I answered under my breath.

For a few moments she was silent. She looked at me however; and as I watched her eyes grow softer I suddenly held out my hand, and for a moment she suffered hers to rest in it. Then she drew away a little.

She was still looking at me steadfastly; but something that had seemed to me inimical had gone from her expression.

"Mr. Walmsley," she said slowly, "I want to tell you I think you are making a mistake. Please listen to me carefully. You do not belong to the order of people from whom the adventurers of the world are drawn. What you are is written in your face. I am perfectly certain you possess the ordinary conventional ideas as to right and wrong - the ideas in which you have been brought up and which have been instilled into you all your life. My father and I belong to a different class of society. There is nothing to be gained for you by mixing with us, and a great deal to be lost."

"May I not judge for myself?" I asked.

"I fear," she answered, looking me full in the face and smiling at me delightfully, "you are just a little prejudiced."

"Supposing," I whispered, "I have discovered something that seems to me better worth living for than anything else I have yet found in the world I know of - if that something belongs to a world in which I have not yet lived - do you blame me if for the sake of it I would be willing to climb down even into - "

She held out her finger warningly. I heard heavy footsteps outside and the rattle of the doorhandle.

"You are very foolish!" she murmured. "Please let my father in."

Mr. Parker returned in high good humor. He had met a host of acquaintances and declared that he had not had a dull moment. As for the performance he seemed to have forgotten there was one going on at all.

"I am for supper," he suggested. "I owe our friend here a supper in return for his interrupted dinner."

"Supper, by all means!" I agreed.

"Remember that I am wearing a hat," Eve said. "We must go to one of the smaller places."

In the end we went back to Stephano's. We sat at the table at which I had so often watched Eve and her father sitting alone, and by her side I listened to the music I had so often heard while I had watched her from what had seemed to me to be an impossible distance.

Mr. Parker talked wonderfully. He spoke of gigantic financial deals in Wall Street; of operations which had altered the policy of nations; of great robberies in New York, the details of which he discussed with amazing technical knowledge.

He played tricks with the knives and forks, balanced the glasses in extraordinary fashion, and reduced our waiters to a state of numbed and amazed incapacity. Every person who entered he seemed to have some slight acquaintance with. All the time he was acknowledging and returning greetings, and all the time he talked.

We spoke finally of gambling; and he laughed heartily when I made mild fun of the gambling scare that was just then being written up in all the papers and magazines.

"So you don't believe in baccarat tables in London!" he said. "Very good! We shall see. After we have supped we shall see!"

We stayed until long past closing time. Mr. Parker continued in the highest good humor, but Eve was subject at times to moods of either indifference or depression. The more intimate note which had once or twice crept into our conversation she seemed now inclined to deprecate. She avoided meeting my eyes.

More than once she glanced toward the clock.

"Haven't you an appointment to-night, father?" she asked, almost in an undertone.

"Sure!" Mr. Parker answered readily. "I have an appointment, and I am going to take you and Mr. Walmsley along."

"I am delighted to hear it!" I exclaimed quickly.

"I'll teach you to make fun of the newspapers," Mr. Parker went on. "No gambling hells in London, eh? Well, we shall see!"

To my great relief Eve made no spoken objection to my inclusion in the party. When at last we left a large and handsome motor car was drawn up outside waiting for us.

"A taxicab," Mr. Parker explained, "is of no use to me - of no more use than a hansom cab. I have to keep a car in order to slip about quietly. Now in what part of London shall we look for a gambling hell, Mr. Walmsley? I know of eleven. Name your own street - somewhere in the West End."

I named one at random.

"The very place!" Mr. Parker declared; "the very place where I have already an appointment. Get in. Say, you Londoners have no idea what goes on in your own city!"

We drove to a quiet street not very far from the Ritz Hotel. Mr. Parker led us across the pavement and we entered a block of flats. The entrance hall was dimly lit and there seemed to be no one about. Mr. Parker, however, rang for a lift, which came promptly down.

"You two will stay here," he directed, "for two or three minutes. Then the lift will come down for you."

He ascended and left us there. I turned at once to Eve, who had scarcely spoken a word during the drive from the restaurant.

"I do wish you would tell me what is troubling you, Miss Parker," I begged. "If I am really in the way of course you have only to say the word and I'll be off at once."

She held my arm for a moment. The touch of her fingers gave me unreasonable pleasure.

"Please don't think me rude or unkind," she pleaded. "Don't even think that I don't like your coming along with us - because I do. It isn't that. Only, as I told my father before supper, you don't belong! You ought not to be seen at these places, and with us. For some absurd reason father seems to have taken a fancy to you. It isn't a very good thing for you. It very likely won't be a good thing for us."

"Do please change your opinion of me a little," I implored her. "I can't help my appearance; but let me assure you I am willing to play the Bohemian to any extent so long as I can be with you. There isn't a thing in your life I wouldn't be content to share," I ventured to add.

She sighed a little petulantly. She was half-convinced,

but against her will.

"You are very obstinate," she declared; "but, of course, you're rather nice."

After that I was ready for anything that might happen. The lift had descended and the porter bade us enter. We stopped at the third floor. In the open doorway of one of the flats Mr. Parker was standing, solid and imposing. He beckoned us, with a broad smile, to follow him.

To my surprise there were no locked doors or burly doorkeepers. We hung up our things in the hall and passed into a long room, in which were some fifteen or twenty people. Most of them were sitting round a *chemin de fer* table; a few were standing at the sideboard eating sandwiches. A dark-haired, dark-eyed, sallow-faced man, a trifle corpulent, undeniably Semitic, who seemed to be in charge of the place, came up and shook hands with Mr. Parker.

"Glad to see you, sir - and your daughter," he said, glancing keenly at them both and then at me. "This gentleman is a friend of yours?"

"Certainly," Mr. Parker replied. "I won't introduce you, but I'll answer for him."

"You would like to play?"

"I will play, certainly," Mr. Parker answered cheerfully. "My friend will watch - for the present, at any rate."

He waved us away, himself taking a seat at the table. I

led Eve to a divan at the farther corner of the room. We sat there and watched the people. There were many whose faces I knew - a sprinkling of stock-brokers, one or two actresses, and half a dozen or so men about town of a dubious type. On the whole the company was scarcely reputable. I looked at Eve and sighed.

"Well, what is it?" she asked.

"This is no sort of place for you, you know," I ventured.

"Here it comes," she laughed; "the real, hidebound, respectable Englishman! I tell you I like it. I like the life; I like the light and shade of it all. I should hate your stiff English country houses, your highly moral amusements, and your dull day-by-day life. Look at those people's faces as they bend over the table!"

"Well, I am looking at them," I told her. "I see nothing but greed. I see no face that has not already lost a great part of its attractiveness."

"Perhaps!" she replied indifferently. "I will grant you that greed is the keynote of this place; yet even that has its interesting side. Where else do you see it so developed? Where else could you see the same emotion actuating a number of very different people in an altogether different manner?"

"For an adventuress," I remarked, "you seem to notice things."

"No one in the world, except those who live by adventures, ever has any inducement to notice things," she retorted. "That is why amateurs are such failures.

One never does anything so well as when one does it for one's living."

"The question is arguable," I submitted.

She shrugged her shoulders.

"Every question is arguable if it is worth while," she agreed carelessly. "Look at all those people coming in!"

"I don't understand it," I confessed. "These places are against the law, yet there seems to be no concealment at all! Why aren't we raided?"

"Raids in this part of London only take place by arrangement," she assured me. "This place will reach its due date sometime, but every one will know all about it beforehand. They are making a clear profit here of about four hundred pounds a night and it has been running for two months now. When the raid comes Mr. Rubenstein - I think that is his name - can pay his five-hundred-pound fine and move on somewhere else. It's wicked - the money they make here some nights!"

"You seem to know a good deal about it," I remarked.

"The place interests father," she told me. "He comes here often."

"And you?"

"Sometimes. I am not always in the humor."

I looked at her long and thoughtfully. Her beauty was

entirely the beauty of a young girl. There were no signs of late hours or anxiety in her face. She puzzled me more than ever.

"I wish I knew," I said, "exactly what you mean when you call yourself an adventuress."

She laughed.

"It means this," she explained: "To-night I have money in my purse, jewels on my fingers, a motor car to ride home in. In a week's time, if things went badly with us, I might have nothing. Then father or I, or both of us, would go out into the world to replenish, and from whomever had most of what we desired we should take as opportunity presented itself."

"Irrespective of the law?"

"Absolutely!"

"Irrespective of your sense of right and wrong?"

"My sense of right and wrong, according to your standards, does not exist."

I gave it up. She seemed thoroughly in earnest, and yet every word she spoke seemed contrary to my instinctive judgment of her. She pointed to the table.

"Look!" she whispered. "These people don't seem as though they had all that money to gamble with, do they? Look! There must be at least a thousand or fifteen hundred pounds upon the table."

It was just as she said these words that the thing

happened. From somewhere among the little crowd of people gathered round the table there came the sound of heavy stamping on the floor, and in less than a moment every light in the room went out. The place was in somber darkness. Then, breaking the momentary silence, there came from outside a shrill whistle. Again there was a silence - and then pandemonium! In a dozen different keys one heard the same shout:

"The police!"

Eve gripped my arm. My matchbox was out in a moment and I struck a match, holding it high over my head. As it burned a queer little halo of light seemed thrown over the table. The door was wide open and blocked with people rushing out. The banker was still sitting in his place. At first I seemed to have the idea that Mr. Parker was by his side. Then, to my astonishment, I saw him at the opposite end of the table, standing as though he had appeared from nowhere. A stentorian voice was heard from outside:

"Ladies and gentlemen, if you please! Nothing has happened. The lights will be on again immediately."

Almost as he spoke the place was flooded with light.

The faces of the people were ghastly. A babel of voices arose.

"Where are the police?"

"Where are they?"

"Who said the police?"

E. Phillips Oppenheim

The little dark gentleman whose name was Rubenstein stood upon a chair.

"Ladies and gentlemen," he called out, "nothing whatever has happened - nothing! The electric lights went out owing to an accident, which I will investigate. It seems to have been a practical joke on the part of the lift man, who has disappeared. There are no police here. Please take your places. The game will proceed."

They came back a little reluctantly, as though still afraid. Then suddenly the banker's hoarse voice rang out through the room. All the time he had been sitting like an automaton. Now he was on his feet, swaying backward and forward, his eyes almost starting from his head.

"Lock the doors! The bank has been robbed! The notes have gone! Mr. Rubenstein, don't let any one go out! I tell you there was two thousand pounds upon the table. Some one has the notes!"

There was a little murmur of voices and a shriek from one of the women as she clutched her handbag. Mr. Parker, bland and benign, rose to his feet.

"My own stake has disappeared," he declared; "and the pile of notes I distinctly saw in front of the banker has gone. I fear, Mr. Rubenstein, there is a thief among us."

Mr. Rubenstein, white as a sheet, was standing at the door. He locked it and put the key in his pocket.

"Ladies and gentlemen," he said, "play is over for to-night. We are, without a doubt, the victims of an attempted robbery. The lights were turned out from the controlling switch by the lift man, who has disappeared. I will ask you to leave the room one by one; and, for all our sakes, I beg that any unknown to us will submit themselves to be searched."

There was a little angry murmur. Mr. Rubenstein looked pleadingly round.

"Ladies and gentlemen," he begged, "you will not object, I am sure. I am a poor man. Two thousand pounds of my money has gone from that table - all the money I kept in reserve to make a bank for you. If any one will return it now nothing shall be said. But to lose it all - I tell you it would ruin me!"

The perspiration stood out on his forehead. He looked anxiously round, as though seeking for sympathy. Mr. Parker came over to his side.

"Say, Mr. Rubenstein," he declared, "there isn't any one here who wants you to lose a five-pound note - that's a sure thing! But there is just one difficulty about this searching business: How can you identify your notes? If I, for instance, were to insist that I had brought with me two thousand pounds in banknotes in my pocket - which, let me hasten to assure you, I didn't - how could you deny it?"

"My notes," Mr. Rubenstein replied feverishly, "all bear the stamp of Lloyd's Bank and to-day's date. They can all be recognized."

"In that case," Mr. Parker continued, "I recommend you, Mr. Rubenstein, to insist upon searching every person here not thoroughly known to you; and I recommend you, ladies and gentlemen," he added, looking round, "to submit to be searched. It will not be a very strenuous affair, because no one can have had time to conceal the notes very effectively. I think you will all agree with me that we cannot allow our friend, who has provided us with amusement for so many nights, to run the risk of a loss like this. Begin with me, Mr. Rubenstein. No - I insist upon it. You know me better than most of your clients, I think; but I submit myself voluntarily to be searched."

"I thank you very much indeed, sir," Mr. Rubenstein declared quickly. "It is very good of you to set the example," he continued, thrusting his hand into Mr. Parker's pockets. "Ah! I see nothing here - nothing! Notes in this pocket - ten, twenty, thirty. Not mine, I see - no Lloyd's stamp. Gold! A pleasant little handful of gold, that. Mr. Parker, I thank you, sir. If you will be so good as to pass into the next room."

I brought Eve up. We were recognized as having been sitting upon the divan and Mr. Rubenstein, with a bow and extended hand, motioned to us to pass on.

"You will visit us again, I trust," he said, "when we are not so disturbed."

"Most certainly!" Mr. Parker promised in our names. "Most certainly, Mr. Rubenstein. We will all come again. Good night!"

We walked out to the landing and, descending the stairs, reached the street and stepped into the motor car that was waiting for us. It rolled off and turned into Piccadilly.

"How much was it, father?" Eve asked suddenly, from her place in the corner.

"I am not sure," Mr. Parker answered. "There is a matter of eight hundred pounds in my right shoe, and a little more than that, I think, in my left. The note down my back was, I believe, a hundred-pound one. Quite a pleasant little evening and fairly remunerative! The lift man will cost me a hundred - but he was worth it."

I sat quite still. I felt that Eve's eyes were watching me. I set my teeth for a moment; and I turned toward her, my cigarette case in my hand.

"You don't mind?" I murmured as I lit a cigarette.

She shook her head. Her eyes were still fixed upon me.

"Where can we drop you?" Mr. Parker inquired.

"If the evening is really over and there are no more excitements to come, you might put me down at the Milan Court," I told him, "if that is anywhere on your way."

Mr. Parker lifted the speaking tube to his lips and gave an order. We glided up to the Milan a few minutes later.

"I have enjoyed my evening immensely," I assured Eve impressively, "every moment of it; and I do hope, Mr. Parker," I added as I shook hands, "that you and your daughter will give me the great pleasure of dining with me any night this week. If there are any other little adventures about here in which I could take a hand I can assure you I should be delighted. I might even be of some assistance."

They both of them looked at me steadfastly. Then Eve at last glanced away, with a little shrug of the shoulders, and Mr. Joseph H. Parker gripped my hand.

"Say, you're all right!" he pronounced. "You just ring up 3771A Gerrard to-morrow morning between ten and eleven."

CHAPTER III

CULLEN GIVES ADVICE

At ten o'clock the following morning my telephone bell rang and a visitor was announced. I did not catch the name given me, and it was only when I opened the door to him in response to his ring that I recognized Mr. Cullen. In morning clothes, which consisted in his case of a blue serge suit that needed brushing and a bowler hat of extinct shape, he seemed to me, if possible, a little more objectionable than I had found him the previous night. He presented himself, however, in a wholly non-aggressive spirit.

"Mr. Walmsley," he said, as he took the chair to which I motioned him, "I have called to see you very largely in your own interests."

I murmured something to the effect that I was extremely obliged.

"I have made inquiries concerning you," he went on, "and I find that you not only have a blameless record but that you are possessed of considerable means, and that you belong to a highly esteemed county family."

"And what of it, Mr. Cullen?" I asked.

"This," he answered, "that I feel it my duty to warn you against the companions with whom you spent a portion of last evening."

"You mean Mr. and Miss Parker?"

"I mean Mr. and Miss Parker."

"Are you making any definite charges against this young lady and gentleman?" I inquired after a moment's pause.

"Very definite charges indeed!" he replied. "I warn you, Mr. Walmsley, that this man and his daughter are in bad repute with us, and to be seen associated with them is to bring yourself under police surveillance. We had a special warning when they sailed from New York, and since their arrival in London they have already been concerned in two or three very shady transactions."

"If they break the law," I inquired, "why do you not arrest them?"

"Because I have had bad luck - rotten bad luck!" Mr. Cullen declared firmly. "I am perfectly convinced that this Mr. Parker, as he calls himself, has been financing one of the greatest artists in banknote counterfeits ever known to the police. I am perfectly convinced that Mr. Parker left this young man in Adam Street last night, with a packet of notes upon his person for which he had just paid two hundred pounds, and if I could have arrested him then the game would have been up. He dodged me by going into the Cecil, leaving by the back way and coming through the Savoy; but I picked him up again within two minutes of his reaching Stephano's.

"Obviously with your collusion - you'll pardon me, sir, but there the facts are - he was seated at your table as though in the middle of a dinner. I had him searched, but there wasn't a thing on him. I am not going to ask you what he did with the notes he had - whether he palmed them off on you or not - but I will simply say that between the time of his entering Stephano's and the time of my searching him he got rid of a thousand pounds' worth of counterfeit notes."

"Sounds very clever of him!" I remarked. "How do you know that he didn't get rid of them to some one in either the Cecil or the Savoy?"

"Because," Mr. Cullen explained, "he was followed by one of my men through both places and not lost sight of for a single second. You see, I made sure he would come to Stephano's and I was on the other side of the Strand, but I had left a man in case he went the other way. I tell you he was under the strictest surveillance the whole time, except during the few minutes - I might almost say seconds - when he disappeared in the restaurant."

"Anything else against him?" I asked.

"I am not inclined," Mr. Cullen continued slowly, "to mention specifically the various cases that have come under my notice and in which I believe him to be concerned; but, among other things, he is a frequenter of half the gambling houses in London and a tout for their owners. Trouble follows wherever he goes. But, Mr. Walmsley, mark my words! I am not a man given to idle speech and I assure you that within a few weeks - perhaps within a few days - I shall have him; aye, and the young lady, too! You don't want to be mixed up in this sort of business, sir. I am here to give you the advice to sheer off! They'll only rob you and bring you, too, under suspicion."

I lit a cigarette and stood on the hearthrug with my hands behind me.

"Mr. Cullen," I said, "it is, of course, very kind of you to come to me in this disinterested manner. You don't seem to have anything to gain by it, so I will accept your attitude as being a bona fide one. I will, if I may, be equally frank with you. I met both Mr. Parker and his daughter last night for the first time - "

"Then that dinner was a plant!" Mr. Cullen interrupted swiftly. "I knew it!"

I ignored the interruption.

"For the first time," I repeated; "and I find them both most delightful companions. As to how far our acquaintance may progress, that is entirely a matter for chance to decide. You have doubtless come here with very good motives, but I see no reason why I should accept your statements concerning Mr. Parker and his daughter. You understand? My suggestion is that you are mistaken. Until I have proved them to be other than they represent themselves to be," I added with infinite subtlety, "I shall continue to derive pleasure from their society."

Mr. Cullen rose at once to his feet.

"My warning has been given, sir," he said. "It only

remains for me now to wish you good morning, and to assure you most regretfully that your name will be added to those whom Scotland Yard thinks it well to watch and that your movements from place to place will be noted."

"I trust that Scotland Yard will benefit," I replied politely, and showed him out.

At half past ten I rang up 3771A Gerrard. The telephone was answered almost immediately by a man, apparently a servant. I inquired for Mr. Parker and in a moment or two I heard his voice at the telephone.

"This is Joseph H. Parker speaking. Who are you?"

"I am Paul Walmsley. You told me I might ring up between ten and eleven."

"Sure!" was the prompt reply. "My dear fellow, I am delighted to hear from you. None the worse for our little adventure last night, I hope?"

"Not in the least," I assured him. "On the contrary I am looking forward to another."

"You shall have one," was the delighted answer.

"What about - What is it, Eve? Excuse me for one moment, Mr. Walmsley."

Mr. Parker was apparently dragged away from the telephone. I waited impatiently. He returned in a moment or two. His voice sounded as though he were a little irritated.

"Sorry," he said. "I was going to make a little suggestion to you for this evening, but my daughter here doesn't fall in with it. They will have their own way - these girls."

"It's very disappointing!" I said. "Don't you think you could prevail on her?"

"Look here!" Mr. Parker continued. "I'll tell you what: Let's meet accidentally at dinner tonight. I'll talk Eve round before then. You drop into Stephano's for dinner at about seven-thirty. Then, when you see us there, you can come over and join us."

"Thank you very much," I replied heartily. "By the by, I suppose you couldn't tell me your address? I should like to send Miss Parker some flowers."

Mr. Parker obviously hesitated.

"Better not," he decided regretfully - "not this morning, at any rate. Eve is a bit peculiar; and if you come into our little scheme and it goes wrong the less you know of us the better. See you later!"

I did see Mr. Parker later, but not quite so late as the time appointed. He was in the American bar at the Milan when I looked in there just before luncheon and was talking to two of the most ferocious and objectionable-looking ruffians I had ever seen in my life. He glanced at me blandly, but without any sign of recognition, save that I fancied I caught the slightest twitch of his left eyebrow. I took the hint and did not join him. My reward came presently; for, after leaving the room with his two acquaintances, Mr. Parker strolled back again, and coming straight over to me clapped me on the shoulder.

"This is capital!" he exclaimed. "We meet tonight?"

"Without a doubt," I assured him.

He drew me a little on one side.

"Say," he inquired, scratching the side of his chin, "have you any objection to a bit of a scrap?"

"Not the slightest," I replied, "so long as Miss Parker is out of it!"

"Good boy!" Mr. Parker pronounced. "Yes; we'll keep her out of it, all right. I shall count on you then. Just keep yourself in reserve. We'll talk it over at dinner time. You just stroll in casually and I'll call you over. By the by," he added, lowering his voice, "did you see those two fellows I was with?"

"I saw them!" I confessed. "They were just a trifle noticeable."

Mr. Parker came a little nearer to me. He accentuated his words by beating on the palm of his left hand with two fingers of his right.

"Absolutely, my dear Walmsley, two of the most unmitigated and desperate ruffians on either continent!"

"They looked it," I agreed heartily.

"Their record," Mr. Parker continued - "their police record, I mean - is one of the most wonderful things

E. Phillips Oppenheim

ever put on paper. The marvelous thing is how, even for a few minutes, they should be out of prison! Did you notice the one with the cast in his eye?"

"I did," I admitted.

"They used to call him Angel Jake," Mr. Parker proceeded confidentially. "He was sentenced to death once for shooting a policeman, but there was some technicality - he was tried in the wrong court - so he got off."

"A very interesting acquaintance," I remarked with utterly wasted sarcasm.

"They're fairly up to their necks in trouble, both of them, on the other side," Mr. Parker declared with relish; "and they're kind o' looking for it here."

I took him by the arm and led him out of the bar into a retired corner of the smoking room. We sat upon a divan and had the room almost to ourselves.

"How is Miss Parker this morning?" I asked.

"Fine!" her father replied. "I told her about the flowers and it made her quite homesick. Girls miss that sort of thing, you know; and over here, living under a sort of cloud, as it were, one can't risk making many friends."

It was a very good opening for me and I took advantage of it.

"Why do you choose to live under a cloud, Mr. Parker?" I asked.

"My dear fellow," he replied earnestly, "I don't altogether choose. I have been frank with you. It's my life."

"If it were only a question of money - " I began tentatively.

"A question of money!" Mr. Parker interrupted. "Isn't everything a question of money? Say, what do you mean exactly?"

"I mean that I admire your daughter, sir - I admire her immensely," I told him. "If she'd have me I'd marry her to-morrow, I am not what you would call a wealthy man, but I have enough money for all reasonable purposes."

Mr. Parker was clearly staggered. He stroked his waistcoat for a moment in an absent sort of way.

"This takes my breath away!" he exclaimed. "Let us understand exactly what it means."

"It means," I told him bluntly, "that I'll make a settlement upon your daughter and give you enough to live on."

He looked first at me and then at the carpet. He began to whistle softly.

"And they always told me," he murmured under his breath, "that you Britishers were so cautious! Why, you know nothing about us at all except what I've told you, and goodness knows that isn't much of a recommendation! Besides, I may not have told you half!"

"I am willing to take my risk," I declared. "I simply don't care. Once in a lifetime a man has that feeling for a woman. If he is wise he goes nap on it. I have never had it before and I am not going to let go. I feel that if I do I may regret it all my life. I don't want any other woman in this world except your daughter, and what I possess in life worth having I am willing to give to make sure of her."

Mr. Parker sat for several moments in profound silence. I could not make out what his mood was, He seemed neither unduly depressed nor elated. He was obviously puzzled, however - puzzled to know precisely what to do or what to say. He sat in the middle of the divan with one thumb in his waistcoat pocket and the other hand flat upon the table. His round face was innocent of smile or frown. Yet I knew he was taking what I had said seriously, though for some reason or other it did not seem to give him unqualified pleasure.

"Well, well!" he said at last. "You've spoken up like a man, anyway - and like a man who knows what he wants. I can't tell how to answer you. I have never lived on any one yet. Sponging's never been in my line. I have enjoyed living on my wits. And Eve - she's a little that way, too. Makes me kind of sorry I've let her go about with me so much. It's a wonderful cloak of respectability you'd throw over us; but I'm wondering whether it's large enough!"

"As my wife - " I began.

"Oh, yes! you'd gather her in all right to start with," he interrupted; "but there are other things," he added, turning a little toward me and looking me in the face.

"Suppose she didn't turn out just as you thought! She's a wild, high-spirited sort of creature - is Eve. She loves the music and the rattle of life. I can't fancy her in one of those out-of-the-way, God-forsaken little mudholes you call an English village, sitting in an early-Victorian drawing-room all the afternoon, waiting for the vicar's wife to come to tea, and taking a walk before dinner for entertainment, with an umbrella and mackintosh."

"You've been reading Jane Austen," I told him.

"Never heard of her," he replied promptly. "I once - but never mind. Just keep this to yourself for a bit, my boy. If we come to any arrangement there are one or two things we've got on that we might have to drop. We'll think this over. So long until this evening."

He bustled away then, evidently anxious to escape any further conversation. I went about my business, which consisted of a visit to my lawyer's and a couple of rubbers of bridge at my club before dinner.

At half past seven precisely I strolled into Stephano's. I had scarcely taken my table before Mr. Parker and Eve entered. Contrary to his usual custom, Mr. Parker was wearing a dress coat, white waistcoat and white tie; and Eve looked exquisite in a low-necked gown of white silk. Mr. Parker, according to his promise, at once beckoned me over.

"My dear boy," he said, "I insist upon it that you sit down and dine with us. Last night I dined with you. To be literal, I ate off your plate. Tonight I return the compliment."

E. Phillips Oppenheim

I had no idea of refusing, but I was watching Eve with some anxiety. Her attitude seemed a little negative. However, she welcomed me pleasantly.

"Well," she asked, "is your conscience beginning to prick yet?"

"My conscience," I replied, "is about as imaginary a thing as my early-Victorian drawing-room. I can assure you I have the most profound admiration for your father. I think he is one of the cleverest men I ever met."

She seemed a little taken aback. My tone, I felt quite sure, was convincing.

"Of course," she remarked, "it is possible I have formed a wrong idea of Englishmen. I have met only one or two."

"I should say it is highly probable," I agreed. "What scheme of villainy is before us to-night? I claim a share in it at any rate."

She shook her head.

"Not to-night, I am afraid."

Mr. Parker, with the menu in front of him, was busy with the waiter and a *maître d'hôtel*. I dropped my voice a little.

"Why not? Are you going to the theater?"

"To the opera."

"You love music?" I asked.

She leaned a little toward me. Her hair almost brushed my cheek as she whispered:

"We love jewelry!"

I flatter myself that not a muscle of my face moved.

"No place like the opera!" I remarked. "You should do well there with a little luck."

This time I certainly scored. She looked at me fixedly for a moment. Then she laughed softly.

"I want a pearl necklace," she said.

"What about the one you have on?"

She held it out toward me.

"Imitations, unfortunately," she sighed. "They may look very nice, but they don't feel like the real thing."

"Why can't I go to the opera with you?" I suggested.

"Because there are no vacant seats anywhere near ours," she replied. "You see we happen to know whom we are going to sit near."

"Anyhow, I think I shall go," I decided, "I may be able to come and talk to you between the acts at any rate."

Mr. Parker, having finished giving his orders, joined in the conversation, and we dined together quite cheerily. For educated Americans they seemed very ignorant of

E. Phillips Oppenheim

English life, and I was not surprised to hear that it was their first visit to Europe. They listened with interest to a great deal that I told them. It was only as we were preparing to leave the place that I asked Mr. Parker a definite question.

"Tell me," I whispered, "have you really any plans for to-night?"

He nodded. "Sure! We are in luck just now. There's nothing like backing it."

"Are those fellows I saw you with this morning at the Milan in it? If so I am going to take Miss Parker away. There are limits - "

He patted me on the back.

"That little affair is off for to-night at any rate. A lady we are very anxious to meet is going to the opera. The little girl wants a pearl necklace. Well, we shall see!"

"You've thought over what I said? Have you mentioned it to her?"

"Only kind of hinted at it. It's no good putting it too straight to her. She's got the bit between her teeth and she'll need to be humored."

Eve had gone to fetch her cloak and we were alone outside the door. I looked at him steadfastly - he was so very pink and white, so very cheerful, so utterly optimistic!

"You've never seen the inside of an English prison, have you, Mr. Parker?" I asked.

He stared at me blankly.

"I am not thinking about you or myself," I went on. "She's so dainty and sweet! She looks like a child who has never known an hour of rough usage in her life. They wouldn't leave her much of that, you know."

I had certainly succeeded in making an impression this time. Mr. Parker's smooth forehead was wrinkled; his face was clouded.

"You are right, Mr. Walmsley," he admitted. "I wish - I wish she would listen to reason. We'll have a talk together - the three of us - soon. You've no idea how difficult it is! She doesn't know fear - can't realize danger. Hush! Here she comes. It will only set her against you if she thinks you are trying to influence me behind her back."

Mr. Parker's car was waiting and we drove together to Covent Garden. I left them in the vestibule and went to call on some of my friends. My sister had a box in the second tier and I was fortunate enough to find her there and alone with her husband. Almost directly underneath us in the stalls Mr. Parker and Eve were sitting; and next Mr. Parker was a woman wearing a pearl necklace. I asked my sister her name. She raised her lorgnette and looked over the side of the box.

"Lady Orstline," she told me. "Her husband is a South African millionaire."

"Are those real pearls she is wearing?" I inquired.

"My dear Paul," she laughed, "why not? Her husband is enormously wealthy and they say that her jewels are wonderful. Unlike so many of those people, she really does select very fine stones, independent of size. Those pearls she is wearing now, for instance, are quite small, but their luster is exquisite. What an extraordinary fat man is sitting next her - and what a pretty girl!"

"Americans," I remarked.

"They look it," she agreed. "Quite the Gibson type of girl, isn't she?"

The curtain went up and we turned our attention to the stage. As a rule I find music soothing; but that night proved an exception - perhaps because my moderately well-ordered life had crumbled into pieces; because I was conscious of a new and overmastering passion - the music appealed to me in an altogether different way. My enjoyment was no longer impersonal - a matter of the brain and the judgment. I felt the excitement of it throbbing in my pulses. The gloomy, half-lit auditorium seemed full of strange suggestions. I felt in real and actual touch with the great things that throbbed beneath. I was no longer an auditor - a looker-on. I had become a participator.

The hours passed as though in a dream. I talked to my sister and her husband, and exchanged the usual gossip with their callers. I even paid a call or two on my own account; but I have no recollection of whom I went to see or what we talked about. I had no chance to visit either Mr. Parker or Eve, for neither of them left their places and they were in the middle of a row; but I took good care that we were close together in the vestibule toward the end. With a little shiver I saw that Lady Orstline was there too - next Mr. Parker. I was a few feet behind them both, with my sister. I found myself watching almost feverishly.

As usual there was a block outside, and the few yards between us and the door seemed interminable. I had none of the optimism of those others. I was filled with vague fears of some impending disaster. Suddenly, with a shiver, I recognized Cullen, scarcely a couple of yards away, also watching, wedged in among the throng. His lips were drawn closely together; his opera hat was well over his forehead; his eyes never left Mr. Parker. He looked to me there like a lean-faced rat preparing for its spring.

I followed the exact direction of his steadfast gaze and I became cold with apprehension. Lady Orstline was just in front of me; by her side was Eve, and immediately behind her Mr. Parker, I tried to lean over, but in the crush it was impossible.

"Some one you want to speak to, Paul?" my sister asked.

"There's a man there - if I can only get at him."

The little crowd in front of us was suddenly thrown into disorder by having to let through two people whose carriage had been called. We seemed to lose ground in the confusion, for a moment or two later I noticed Lady Orstline standing outside the door, and my heart sank as I realized that her neck was bare. Almost at the same instant I saw her hand fly up and heard her voice.

"My necklace!" she called out. "Policeman, don't let any one pass out! My necklace has been stolen - my pearls!"

E. Phillips Oppenheim

The confusion that followed was indescribable. The doors were almost barricaded. My sister and her husband and I were allowed through easily enough, as we were known to be subscribers, but almost every one else seemed to be undergoing a sort of crossexamination. My brother-in-law was disposed to be irritable.

"Why can't the silly woman look after her jewels?" he exclaimed. "Another advertisement, I suppose."

"Can we drop you anywhere, Paul?" my sister inquired. "Or would you like to give us some supper?"

I had been staring out of the window. There was not a sign anywhere of Eve or her father; nor had I been able to catch a glimpse of Mr. Cullen.

"I am sorry," I replied; "but I am supping with some friends at Stephano's. Could you set me down there?"

My sister raised her eyebrows as she gave the order. We were already in the Strand.

"Really, Paul," she remonstrated, "at your time of life - you are thirty-four years old, mind - I think you might leave Stephano's to the other generation!"

"Second childhood!" I explained as I descended. "In any case I really have an appointment here. Give you supper any other night with pleasure. Many thanks!"

My first intention had been not to enter the place at all, but to return at once to Covent Garden. Some impulse, however, prompted me to glance round the room first. To my amazement Eve and her father were already seated at their usual table - Eve drawing off her gloves and her father with the wine list in his hand. I made my way toward them. I suppose my expression indicated a certain stupefaction, for directly I got there Eve began to laugh softly up into my face.

"We aren't ghosts!" she declared. "Did you think *you* were the only person who could leave the opera house in a hurry?"

"I saw you in the vestibule," I ventured. "I never saw you get away."

"No more did our friend Cullen," Mr. Parker remarked, smiling. "I really am beginning to feel sorry for that man. We were within a yard or two of him and he was watching us good and hard. I think he had an idea that Eve had a weakness for pearls."

"Oh, don't!" I exclaimed rather sharply. "Even in joke it isn't exactly wise, is it, with people passing all the time?"

"Joke!" Mr. Parker repeated. "Precious little joke about it, I can assure you. I dare say it looked simple enough to you, but it was really quite a complicated business. Never mind, Eve has her pearls - and that's the great thing."

Then he thrust his hand into his trousers pocket and, without the least attempt at concealment, produced and plumped upon the table in front of him the pearl necklace which only a few minutes before I had seen upon the neck of Lady Orstline.

"Look much better on Eve when they've been

re-strung, won't they?" he observed. "Gee whiz! What lovely stones they are!"

"Put it away!" I gasped. "For Heaven's sake, put it away!"

"Why should I?" he asked coolly.

My heart suddenly seemed to stop beating. I felt as though the end of the world had come. With the light of triumph ablaze in his narrow black eyes,
Mr. Cullen was standing by our table!

"Good evening, Mr. Parker!" he said in a tone from which he struggled to keep the note of triumph. "Good evening, young lady!"

The hand of Mr. Parker had suddenly covered the pearl necklace. Mr. Cullen was looking steadily toward it.

"I trust," he continued, "that my arrival was not inopportune. I haven't interrupted anything, have I - any little celebration, or anything of that sort?"

"On the contrary, we are always pleased to see you," Mr. Parker declared warmly. "Sit right down, Mr. Cullen! You'll join us, I trust? We were just thinking of ordering a little supper."

Mr. Cullen shook his head. "Perhaps," he advised, "it would be better to postpone that order."

"Postpone it?" Mr. Parker repeated, glancing at the clock. "Why, it's late enough now. Good Heavens, is that the time?"

Mr. Cullen and I both glanced at the clock at the other end of the room. It was twenty minutes to twelve. The detective looked back with a smile.

"You are a past master, Mr. Parker," he said, "in the accomplishment that, I believe, in your country goes by the name of bluff; but there are limits, you know. I shall have to ask you and your daughter and Mr. Walmsley here to accompany me at once to Bow Street. And," he added, suddenly leaning across the table, "move your right hand, please! Don't make a disturbance - for Luigi's sake! If you want trouble you can have it."

Mr. Parker raised his hand at once.

"Trouble?" he echoed. "That's the last thing I'm looking for."

Mr. Cullen smiled grimly.

"Ah! I thank you," he said. "A pearl necklace, I see! You must allow me to take charge of this, please."

Mr. Parker's look of surprise was admirably done.

"That is my daughter's necklace," he explained. "The fastening has become loose."

"Exactly!" Mr. Cullen sneered. "I am now going to ask you all three to come with me without any further delay to Bow Street."

"This man is mad!" Mr. Parker sighed, leaning back in his place - "stark, staring mad! His interference with my meals is becoming unwarrantable."

"If you take my advice you will avoid a scene," the detective said, leaning a little over the table. "Believe me, I am not to be trifled with. If you do not come willingly there are other means. I am simply trying to avoid a disturbance in a public restaurant."

Mr. Parker rose reluctantly to his feet.

"Eve, dear," he said, "I suppose we may as well obey this very autocratic person. The sooner we go the sooner we shall be back to supper. Mr. Walmsley, I owe you my most profound apologies. I had no idea when I asked you to join us that you would become involved in anything disagreeable."

"Don't mind me," I begged him. "I am glad to come. Perhaps we had better get it over as soon as possible."

"We shall be back," Mr. Parker explained to Luigi, who had strolled up to see what was happening, "in twenty minutes. Prepare, if you please, three oyster cocktails, some grilled cutlets, and sauté potatoes. Thank you, Luigi. In twenty minutes, mind!"

We passed out toward the entrance. Mr. Cullen was walking with almost professional proximity to his companion. Eve and I were a few steps in the rear.

"Eve," I whispered, drawing her for a moment close to me, "remember that whatever comes of this - whatever happens - there is no word I have ever said to you, or to your father about you, which I do not mean and shall not always mean."

She looked at me a little curiously. From the first her own demeanor had been singularly unmoved. During the last few seconds, however, she had grown paler. She suddenly took my hand and gave it a little squeeze.

"You really are a little more than nice!" she said.

We drove to the police station and Mr. Cullen ushered us at once into a private room, where an inspector was seated at a table.

"Mr. Hennessey, sir," he began, "I have a charge of theft against this man and his daughter. I watched them at the opera house to-night. At the entrance they were both of them hustling Lady Orstline. As you may have heard, she cried out suddenly that her pearl necklace had been stolen. I rushed for these two, but by some means or other they got away. I followed them to Stephano's restaurant and discovered them with the necklace on the table in front of them; The man Parker was showing it to the other two. He attempted to conceal it, but I was just in time."

The inspector nodded.

"Very good, Mr. Cullen," he said. "Where is the necklace?"

The detective produced it proudly and laid it upon the table before him. The inspector dipped his pen in the ink.

"What is your name?" he asked Mr. Parker.

"Joseph H. Parker," was the reply. "I am an American citizen and this is my daughter. Mr. Cullen appears to be a person of observation. It is true we were at the opera. It is perfectly true we were within a few yards of Lady Orstline when she called out that her necklace was stolen. There's nothing remarkable about that, however, as we occupied adjacent stalls. What I want to point out to you is, though, if you'll allow me, that the necklace I had on the table before me at Stephano's when Mr. Cullen suddenly popped round the screen - the necklace you are now looking at, sir - is of imitation pearls, valued at about ten pounds. I bought it in the Burlington Arcade; it belongs to my daughter, and I was simply examining the clasp, which is scarcely safe."

There was a moment's breathless silence. To me Mr. Parker's statement seemed too good to be true; yet he had spoken with the easy confidence of a man who knows what he is about. Standing there, the personification of respectability, a trifle indignant, a trifle contemptuous, his words could not fail to carry with them a certain amount of conviction. The inspector rang a bell by his side.

"What are your daughter's initials?" he asked quickly.

"E.P. - Eve Parker," Mr. Parker replied. "Look at the back of the gold clasp. There you are," he pointed out - "E.P."

Mr. Cullen and the inspector both bent over the necklace. The inspector gave a brief order to a policeman.

"The initials on the clasp are certainly E.P.," the inspector admitted slowly. "I do not pretend to be a judge of jewelry myself. However, I have sent for some one who is."

A man in plain clothes entered the room. The inspector beckoned to him, showed him the necklace and whispered a question. The man examined the pearls for barely five seconds. Then he handed them back.

"Very nice imitation, sir," he pronounced. "There's a place in Bond Street where I should imagine these came from, and another in the Burlington Arcade. Their value is from seven to ten pounds."

The inspector dismissed him. He handed the necklace back to Mr. Parker and rose to his feet.

"I can only express my most profound regret, sir," he said, "on behalf, of the force. Such a mistake is inexcusable. Mr. Cullen will, I am sure, join in offering you every apology."

Mr. Cullen was standing a few yards back. He was biting his lip until it was absolutely colorless. There was a look in his face that was quite indescribable.

"If I have made a mistake this time," he muttered; "if I have been premature - I apologize; but - but - "

Mr. Parker turned to the inspector.

"You know," he said, "I fancy this young man's got what they call on this side a 'down' on me! He's got an idea that I'm a crook - follows me about; doesn't give me a moment's peace, in fact. Say, Mr. Inspector, can't I put this thing right somehow - take him to my banker's - "

"Banker's!" Mr. Cullen ejaculated softly. "The only use you have for a banker is to fleece him!"

"Mr. Cullen!" the inspector exclaimed, frowning.

"I beg your pardon, sir. I am sorry if I forgot myself." He turned abruptly toward the door. "I offer you my apologies, Mr. Parker," he said, looking back; "also the young lady. But - some day the luck may be on my side."

The door slammed behind him. Mr. Parker turned toward the inspector.

"That young man, Mr. Inspector," he said complainingly, "puts altogether too much feeling into his work. I may have been a bit sarcastic with him once or twice; but if it comes to a lifelong vendetta, or anything of that sort, why, he's beginning to look for trouble - that's all! I'm getting sick of the sight of him. If ever I lunch or dine out he's there. If I go to a theater he's about. Whatever harmless amusement I go in for he's there looking on. Just give him a word of caution, Mr. Inspector. I'm a good-tempered man, but this can't go on forever."

The inspector himself escorted us to the door.

"I beg, Mr. Parker," he said, "that you will take no more notice of Mr. Cullen's little fit of temper. As regards your complaint, I promise you that I will talk to him seriously. Allow me to send for a taxicab for you. Oh! I beg your pardon - that is your own car. I only regret that we should have wasted a few minutes of your evening. Good night, gentlemen! Good night, madam!"

We left Bow Street amid many manifestations of courtesy and good will.

"Where shall I tell him to go to, sir?" the policeman asked as he closed the door.

"Back to Stephano's!" Mr. Parker ordered.

We glided down into the Strand. Mr. Parker glanced at his watch.

"We shall just about make those grilled cutlets," he remarked. "Gives you kind of an appetite - this sort of thing! Say, what's the matter with you, Mr. Walmsley?"

"Oh, nothing particular!" I answered. "Only I was just wondering what in the name of all that's miraculous can have become of Lady Orstline's necklace!"

We descended at Stephano's and were ushered to our table, where the oyster cocktails were waiting. Mr. Parker took my arm.

"Perhaps," he murmured, "you may even know that before you go to sleep to-night."

* * * * *

I thought of Mr. Parker's words an hour or so later when I was preparing to undress. I emptied first the things from my trousers pockets. The feeling of something unfamiliar in one of them brought a puzzled exclamation to my lips. I dragged it out and held it in front of me. My heart gave a great leap, the perspiration broke out upon my forehead, My knees shook and I sat down on the bed. Without the slightest doubt in the world it was Lady Orstline's pearl necklace!

E. Phillips Oppenheim

CHAPTER IV

THE WOOING OF EVE

I spent a very restless and disturbed night. I rose at six o'clock the following morning, and at ten o'clock I rang up 3771A Gerrard. My inquiry was answered almost at once by Mr. Parker himself.

"Is that you, Walmsley?"

"It is," I replied. "I have been waiting to ring you up since daylight! I want you to understand - "

"You come right round here!" Mr. Parker interrupted soothingly. "No good getting fussy over the telephone!"

"Where to?" I asked. "You forget I don't know your address. I should have been round hours ago if I had known where to find you."

"Bless my soul, no more you do! We are at Number 17, Banton Street - just off Oxford Street, you know."

"I am coming straightaway," I replied.

I was there within ten minutes. The place seemed to be a sort of private hotel, unostentatious and unprepossessing. A hall porter, whose uniform had seen better days and whose linen had seen cleaner ones, conducted me to the first floor. Mr. Parker himself met me on the landing.

"Come right in!" he invited. "I saw you drive up. Eve is in there."

He ushered me into a large sitting room of the type one would expect to find in such a place, but which, by dint of many cushions, flowers, and feminine knickknacks, had been made to look presentable. Eve was seated in an easy-chair by the fire. She turned round at my entrance and laughed.

"Where's my necklace, please?" she demanded.

"The necklace," I replied, as severely as I could, "is by this time on its way to Lady Orstline - if it is not actually in her hands."

"You mean to say you have sent it back?" Mr. Parker exclaimed incredulously.

"Certainly!" I replied. "I posted it to her early this morning."

Mr. Parker's expression was one of blank bewilderment.

"Say, do I understand you rightly?" he continued, coming up and laying his great hand upon my shoulder. "You mean to say that, after all we went through because of that miserable necklace, you've gone and chucked it? Do you know it was worth twenty-five thousand pounds?"

"I don't care whether it was worth twenty-five thousand pounds or twenty-five thousand pennies!" retorted I. "It belonged to Lady Orstline - not to you or your daughter or to me. I know that you are a skillful conjurer and I won't ask you how it found its way into my pocket. I am only glad I have had an opportunity of returning it to its owner."

Mr. Parker shook his head ponderously. He turned to Eve.

"This," he said solemnly, "is the young man who asked leave to join us! What do you think of him, Eve?"

"Nothing at all!" she replied flippantly. "He is absolutely useless!"

"If you think," Mr. Parker went on, "we are in this business for our health, I want you to understand right here that you are mistaken. I never deceived you. I told you the first few seconds we met that I was an adventurer. I am. I brought off a coup last night with that necklace, and you've gone and queered it! It isn't for myself I mind so much," he concluded, "but there's the child there, I was going to have the pearls restrung and let her wear them a bit - until the time came for selling them."

"Look here!" I said. "Let us understand one another. It's all very well to live by your wits; to make a little out of people not quite so smart as you are; to worry through life owing a little here and there, borrowing a bit where you can and taking good care to be on the right side when there's a bargain going. That, I take it, is more or less what is meant by being an adventurer. But when it comes to downright thieving I protest! The penalties are too severe. I beg you, Mr. Parker, to have nothing more to do with it!"

I went on, speaking as earnestly as I could and laying my hand upon his shoulder.

"I ask you now what I asked you yesterday: Give me your daughter! Or if I can't win her all at once let me at any rate have the opportunity of meeting her and trying to persuade her to be my wife. I promise you you shan't have to do any of these things for a living - either of you. Be sensible, Miss Parker - Eve!" I begged, turning to her; "and please be a little kind. I am in earnest about this. Come on my side and help me persuade your father. I am not wealthy, perhaps, as you people count money, but I am not a poor man. I'll buy you some pearls."

Eve threw down the book she had been reading and leaned over the side of her chair, looking at me. She seemed no longer angry. There was, indeed, a touch of that softness in her face which I had noticed once before and which had encouraged me to hope. Her forehead was a little puckered, her dear eyes a little wistful. She looked at me very earnestly; but when I would have moved toward her she held out her hand to keep me back.

"You know," she said, "I think you are quite nice, Mr. Walmsley. I rather like this outspoken sort of love-making. It's quite out of date, of course; but it reminds me of Mrs. Henry Wood and crinolines and woolwork, and all that sort of thing. Anyhow, I like it and - I rather like you, too. But, you see, it's how long? - a matter of thirty-six hours since I met you first! Now I couldn't make up my mind to settle down for life with a man I'd only known thirty-six hours, even if he is rash enough to offer to pension my father and remove me from a life of crime."

"The circumstances," I persisted, "are exceptional. You may laugh at it as much as you like; but there are very excellent reasons why you should be taken away from this sort of life."

She shrugged her shoulders a little dubiously.

"There again!" she protested. "I am not so sure that I want to be taken away from it. I like adventures - I adore excitement; in fact I must have it."

"You shall," I promised. "I'll take you to Paris and Monte Carlo. We'll go up to Khartum and take a caravan beyond. You shall go big-game shooting with me in Africa. I'll take you where very few women have been before. I'll take you where you can gamble with life and death instead of this sordid business of freedom or prison. We'll start for Abyssinia in three weeks if you like. I'll find you excitement - the right sort. I'll take you into the big places, where one feels - and the empty places, where one suffers."

Her eyes flashed sympathetically for a moment.

"It sounds good," she admitted, "and yet - am I ungrateful, I wonder? - there's no excitement for me except where men and women are. I'm afraid I'm a daughter of Babylon."

"Doomed from her infancy to a life of crime, I fear," Mr. Parker declared, pinching a cigar he had just taken out of a box. "She loves the rapier play - the struggle with men and women. Takes risks every moment of the time and thrives on it. All the same, Mr. Walmsley, there's something very attractive about the way you are talking. I am not going to let my little girl decide too hastily. Our sort of life's all very well when we are number one and Mr. Cullen's number two. We can't have the luck all the time, though."

"I haven't dared to mention it in plain words," I answered, "because the thought, the mere thought, of what might happen to Miss Eve is too horrible! But the risk is there all the time. One doesn't deal in forged notes or steal pearl necklaces for nothing; and you've an enemy in Cullen if ever any one had. He means to get you both, and if you give him the least chance he'll have no mercy."

I looked at them anxiously. The whole thing seemed to me so momentous. Neither of them showed the slightest signs of fear or apprehension. Mr. Parker, with his newly lit cigar in the corner of his mouth, was smiling a smile of pleasant contentment. Eve, leaning back in her chair, with her hands clasped round the back of her head, was gazing at me with a bewitching little smile on her lips.

"I am not a bit afraid of Mr. Cullen," she declared softly.

"Between you and me," her father remarked, knocking the ash from his cigar, "there's only one darned thing in this world we are afraid of and that, thank the Lord, isn't this side of the Atlantic!"

The smile faded from Eve's lips. For a moment she closed her eyes - a shiver passed through her frame.

E. Phillips Oppenheim

"Don't!" she begged weakly.

"I guess I'll leave it at that," her father agreed. "Now this little proposition of yours, Mr. Walmsley, has just got to lie by for a little time - perhaps only for a very short time. It's a kind of business for us to make up our minds to part with our liberty or any portion of it. Meanwhile, if you'd like to take Eve for a motor ride round and meet me for luncheon, why, the car's outside, and if Eve's agreeable I can pass the time all right."

I looked at her eagerly. She rose at once to her feet.

"Why, it would be charming, if you have nothing to do, Mr. Walmsley," she assented. "I'll put my hat on at once."

"I have nothing to do at any time now but to respect your wishes," I answered firmly, "and wait until you are sensible enough to say Yes to my little proposition."

She looked back at me from the door with a twinkle in her eyes.

"You know," she said, "before I came over I was told that Englishmen were rather slow. I shall begin to doubt it. You wouldn't describe yourself exactly as shy, would you, Mr. Walmsley?"

"I don't know about that," I replied; "but we have other traits as well. We know what we want; very often we get it."

Mr. Parker rose to his feet. He put his hand on my

shoulder. He was the very prototype of the self-respecting, conscientious, prospective father-in-law.

"Young fellow," he confessed, "I shall end by liking you!" I drove with Eve for about two hours. We went out nearly as far as Kingston and wound up in the heart of the West End. I tried to persuade her to walk down Bond Street, but she shook her head.

"To tell you the truth," she confided, "I am not very fond of being seen upon the streets. You know how marvelously clever dad is; still we have been talked about once or twice, and there are several people whom I shouldn't care about meeting."

I sighed as I looked out of the window toward the jewelers' shops.

"I should very much like," I said, "to buy you an engagement ring."

She laughed at me.

"You absurd person! Why, I am not engaged to you yet!"

"You are very near it," I assured her. "Anyhow, it would be an awfully good opportunity for you to show me the sort of ring you like."

She shook her head.

"Not to-day," she decided. "Somehow or other I feel that if ever I do let you, you'll choose just the sort of ring I shall love, without my interfering. Where did we say we'd pick father up?"

"Here," I answered, as the car came to a standstill outside the Café Royal. "I'll go in and fetch him."

I found Mr. Parker seated at a table with two of the most villainous specimens of humanity I had ever beheld. They were of the same class as the men with whom he had been talking at the Milan, but still more disreputable. He welcomed me, however, without embarrassment.

"Just passing the time, my dear fellow!" he remarked airily. "Met a couple of acquaintances of mine. Will you join us?"

"Miss Parker is outside in the car," I explained. "If you don't mind I will go out and wait with her. You can join us when you are ready."

"Five minutes - not a moment longer, I promise!" he called out after me. "Sorry you won't join us."

I took my place once more by Eve's side. Perhaps my tone was a little annoyed.

"Your father is in there," I said, "with two of the most disreputable-looking ruffians I have ever seen crawling upon the face of the earth. What in the world induces him to sit at the same table with them I cannot imagine."

"Necessity, perhaps," she remarked. "Very likely they are highly useful members of our industry."

Mr. Parker came out almost immediately afterward. I suggested the Ritz for luncheon. They looked at each other dubiously.

"To be perfectly frank with you, my dear fellow," Mr. Parker explained, as he clambered into the car and took the place I had vacated by his daughter's side, "it would give us no pleasure to go to the Ritz. We have courage, both of us - my daughter and I - as you may have observed for yourself; but courage is a different thing from rashness. We have been enjoying a very pleasant and not unlucrative time for the last six weeks, with the - er - natural result that there are several ladies and gentlemen in London whom I would just as soon avoid. The Ritz is one of those places where one might easily come across them."

"The Carlton? Prince's? Claridge's? Berkeley?" I suggested. "Or what do you say to Jules' or the Milan grill-room?"

Mr. Parker shook his head slowly.

"If you really mean that you wish me to choose," he said, "I say Stephano's."

"As you will," I agreed. "I only suggested the other places because I thought Miss Parker might like a change."

We drove to Stephano's. It struck me that Luigi's greeting was scarcely so cordial as usual. He piloted us, however, to the table usually occupied by Mr. Parker. On the way he took the opportunity of drawing me a little apart.

"Mr. Walmsley, sir," he said, "can you tell me anything about Mr. Parker and his daughter?"

"Anything about them?" I repeated.

"That they are Americans I know," he continued, "and that the young lady is beautiful - well, one has eyes! It is not my business to be too particular as to the character of those who frequent my restaurant; but twice Mr. Parker has been followed here by a detective, and last night, as you know, they left practically under arrest. It is not good for my restaurant, Mr. Walmsley, to have the police so often about, and if Mr. Parker and his daughter are really of the order of those who pass their life under police supervision, I would rather they patronized another restaurant."

I only laughed at him.

"My dear Luigi," I protested, "be careful how you turn away custom. Mr. Parker is, I should think, no better or any worse than a great many of your clients."

"If one could but keep the police out of it!" Luigi observed. "Could you drop a word to the gentleman, sir? Since I have seen them in your company I have naturally more confidence, but it is not good for my restaurant to have it watched by the police all the time."

"I'll see what can be done, Luigi," I promised him.

Mr. Parker was twice called up on the telephone during luncheon time. He seemed throughout the meal preoccupied; and more than once, with a word of apology to me, he and Eve exchanged confidential whispers. I felt certain that something was in the air, some new adventure from which I was excluded, and my heart sank as I thought of all the grim possibilities overshadowing it.

I watched them with their heads close together, Mr. Parker apparently unfolding the details of some scheme; and it seemed to me that, after all, the wisest thing I could do was to bid this strange pair farewell after luncheon and return either to the country or cross over to Paris for a few days. And then a chance word, a little look from Eve, a little touch from her fingers, as it occurred to her that I was being neglected, made me realize the absolute impossibility of doing anything of the sort.

For a person of my habits of life and temperament I had certainly fallen into a strange adventure. Not only had Eve herself come to mean for me everything that was real and vital in life, but I was most curiously attracted by her terrible father. I liked him.

I liked being with him. He was a type of person I had never met before in my life and one whom I thoroughly appreciated. I sat and watched him during an interval of the conversation.

Geniality and humor were stamped upon his expression. "I am enjoying life!" he seemed to say to everybody. "Come and enjoy it with me!" What a man to be walking the tight rope all the time - to be risking his character and his freedom day by day!

"If there is anything more on hand," I said, trying to make my tone as little dejected as possible, "I should like to be in it."

Mr. Parker scratched his chin.

"I am not sure that you really enjoy these little episodes."

"Of course I don't enjoy them," I admitted indignantly. "You know that. I hate them. I am miserable all the time, simply because of what may happen to you and to Miss Eve."

Mr. Parker sighed.

"There you are, you see!" he declared. "That's the one kink in your disposition, sir, which places you irrevocably outside the class to which Eve and I belong. Now let me ask you this, young man," he went on: "What is the most dangerous thing you've ever done?"

"I've played some tough polo," I remembered.

"That'll do," Mr. Parker declared. "Now tell me: When you turned out you knew perfectly well that a broken leg or a broken arm - perhaps a cracked skull - was a distinct possibility. Did you think about this when you went into the game? Did you think about it while you were playing?"

"Of course I didn't," I admitted.

"Just so!" Mr. Parker concluded triumphantly. "That's where the sporting instinct comes in. You know a thing is going to amuse and excite you. Beyond that you do not think."

"But in this case," I persisted, "I think it is your duty to think for your daughter's sake."

Eve flashed upon me the first angry glance I had seen from her.

"I think," she decided coldly, "it is not worth while discussing this matter with Mr. Walmsley. We are too far apart in our ideas. He has been brought up among a different class of people and in a different way. Besides, he misses the chief point. If I weren't an adventuress, Mr. Walmsley, I might have to become a typist and daddy might have to serve in a shop. Don't you think that we'd rather live - really live, mind - even for a week or two of our lives, than spend dull years, as we have done, upon the treadmill?"

"I give it up," I said. "There is only one argument left. You know quite well that the pecuniary excuse exists no longer."

She looked at me and her face softened.

"You are a queer person!" she murmured. "You are so very English, so very set in your views, so very respectable; and yet you are willing to take us both - "

"I am only thinking of marrying you," I interrupted.

"Well, you were going to make daddy an allowance, weren't you?"

"With great pleasure," I assured her vigorously; "and I only wish you'd take my hand now and we'd fix up everything to-morrow. We could go down and see my house in the country, Eve - I think you'd love it - and there are such things, even in England, you know, as special licenses."

"You dear person!" she laughed. "I can't be rushed into respectability like this."

Perhaps that was really my first moment of genuine encouragement, for there had been a little break in her voice, something in her tone not altogether natural. If only we had been alone - if even another summons to the telephone had come just then for her father! Fortune, however, was not on my side. Instead, the waiter appeared with the bill and diverted my attention. Eve and her father whispered together. The moment had passed.

"Anything particular on this afternoon, Walmsley? "Mr. Parker asked as he rose to his feet.

"Not a thing," I replied.

"I have just got to hurry off," he explained; "a little matter of business. Eve has nothing to do for an hour or so - "

"I'll look after her if I may," I interposed eagerly.

"Don't be later than half past five, Eve," her father directed as he went off, "and don't be tired."

We followed him a few minutes later into the street. A threatening shower had passed away. The sky over-head was wonderfully soft and blue; the air was filled with sunlight, fragrant with the perfume of barrows of lilac drawn up in the gutter. Eve walked by my side, her head a little thrown back, her eyes for a moment half closed.

"But London is delicious on days like this!" she exclaimed. "What are you going to do with me, Mr. Walmsley?"

"Take you down to the Archbishop of Canterbury and marry you!" I threatened.

She shook her head.

"I couldn't be married on a Friday! Let us go and see some pictures instead."

We went into the National Gallery and wandered round for an hour. She knew a great deal more about the pictures than I did, and more than once made me sit down by her side to look at one of her favorite masterpieces.

"I want to go to Bond Street now," she said when we left, "I think it will be quite all right at this time in the afternoon, and there are some weird things to be seen there. Do you mind?"

We walked again along Pall Mall. Passing the Carlton she suddenly clutched at my arm. A little stifled cry escaped her; the color left her cheeks. We increased our speed. Presently she breathed a sigh of relief.

"Heavens, what an escape!" she exclaimed. "Do you think he saw me?"

"Do you mean the young man who was getting out of the taxicab?"

She nodded.

"One of our victims," she murmured; "daddy's victim, rather. I didn't do a thing to him."

"I am quite sure he didn't see you," I told her. "He was

struggling to find change."

She sighed once more. The incident seemed to have shaken her.

"The worst of our sort of life is," she confided, "that it must soon come to an end. We have victims all over the place! One of them is bound to turn up and be disagreeable sooner or later."

"I should say, then," I remarked, "that the moment is opportune for a registrar's office and a trip to Abyssinia."

"And leave daddy to face the music alone?" she objected. "It couldn't be done."

We turned into a tea shop and sat in a remote corner of the place. I had made up my mind to say no more to her that day, but the opportunity was irresistible.

There was a little desultory music, a hum of distant conversation, and Eve herself was thoughtful. I pleaded with her earnestly.

"Eve," I begged, "if only you would listen to me seriously! I simply cannot bear the thought of the danger you are in all the time. Give it up, dear, this moment - to-day! We'll lead any sort of life you like. We'll wander all over Europe - America, if you say the word. I am quite well enough off to take you anywhere you choose to go and still see that your father is quite comfortable. You've made such a difference in such a short time!"

She was certainly quieter and her tone was softer. She

avoided looking at me.

"Perhaps," she said very gently, "this feeling you speak of would pass away just as quickly."

"There isn't any fear of that!" I assured her. "As I care for you now, Eve, I must care for you always; and you know it's torture for me to think of you in trouble - perhaps in disgrace. As my wife you shall be safe. You'll have me always there to protect you. I should like to take you even farther afield for a time - to India or Japan, if you like - and then come back and start life all over again."

"You're rather a dear!" she murmured softly. "I will tell you something at any rate. I do care for you - a little - better than I've ever cared for any one else; but I can't decide quite so quickly."

"Give up this adventure to-night!" I begged. "I hate to mention it, Eve, but if money - I put my checkbook in my pocket to-day. If your father would only - "

She stopped me firmly.

"After the things you have told me," she said, "I don't think I could bear to have him take your money to-day. I can't quite do as you wish; but what you have said shall make a difference, I promise you. I can't say more. Please drive me home now."

CHAPTER V

MR. SAMUELSON

The moment I opened my paper the next morning the very announcement I had dreaded to find was there in large type! I read the particulars breathlessly: DARING BURGLARY IN HAMPSTEAD - LADY LOSES TWO THOUSAND POUNDS' WORTH OF JEWELRY. The burglary had taken place at the house of a Mr. and Mrs. Samuelson, in Wood Grove, Hampstead. It appeared that a dinner party had been given at the house during the evening, which had engaged the attention of the whole of the staff of four servants, and that for an hour or so the upper premises were untenanted.

Upon retiring to rest Mrs. Samuelson found that her jewel case and the whole of her jewelry, except what she was wearing, had been stolen. As no arrest had yet been made the references to the affair were naturally guarded. The paragraph even concluded without the usual formula as to the police having a clew. On the whole, I put the paper down with a slight feeling of relief. I felt that it might have been worse.

I breakfasted at nine o'clock, after having read the announcement through again, trying to see whether there was any possible connection between it and my friends. Then I lit a pipe and sat down to wait until I could ring up 3771A Gerrard. About ten o'clock, however, my own telephone bell rang, and I was informed that a gentleman who desired to see me was waiting below. I told the man to send him up, and in a moment or two there was a knock at my door. In response to my invitation to enter a short, dark, Jewish-looking person, with olive complexion, shiny black hair and black mustache, presented himself. He carried a very immaculate silk hat and was dressed with great neatness. He had the air, however, of a man who is suffering from some agitation.

"Mr. Walmsley, I believe?" he asked. "Mr. Paul Walmsley?"

"That is my name."

"Know you by hearsay quite well, sir," my visitor assured me, with a flash of his white teeth. "Very glad to meet you indeed. I have done business once or twice with your sister, the Countess of Aynesley - business in curios. You know my place, I dare say, in St. James Street. My name is Samuelson." I could scarcely repress a little start, which he was quick to notice. "Perhaps you've been reading about that affair at my house last night?" he asked.

"That is precisely what I have been doing," I admitted. "Please sit down, Mr. Samuelson." I wheeled an easy-chair up for him and placed a box of cigarettes at his elbow. "Quite a mysterious affair!" I continued. "It is almost the first burglary I have ever read of in which the police have not been said to possess a clew."

Mr. Samuelson, who seemed gratified by his reception,

lit a cigarette and crossed his legs, displaying a very nice pair of patent boots, with gray suède tops.

"It is a very queer affair, indeed," he told me confidentially. "The police have been taking a lot of trouble about it, and a very intelligent sort of fellow from Scotland Yard has been in and out of the house ever since."

"Any clew at all?" I asked.

"Rather hard to say," Mr. Samuelson replied. "You'll be wondering what I've come to see you about. Well, I'll just explain. Of course there's always the chance that some one may have entered the house while we were all at dinner - crept upstairs quietly and got away with the jewel case; but this Johnny I was telling you about, from Scotland Yard, seems to have got hold of a theory that has rather knocked me of a heap. Very delicate matter," Mr. Samuelson continued, "as you will understand when I tell you that he thinks it may have been one of my guests who was in the show."

"Seems a little far-fetched to me," I remarked; "but one never knows."

"You see," Mr. Samuelson explained, "there's no back exit from my house without climbing walls and that sort of thing, and it happened to be a particularly light evening, as you may remember. There are policemen at both ends of the road, who seem unusually confident that no one carrying a parcel of any sort passed at anything like the time when the thing was probably done. This is where the Johnny from Scotland Yard comes in. He has got the idea into his head that the jewels might have been taken away in the carriage of one of my guests."

"Well," I remarked, "I should have thought you would have been the best judge as to the probability of that. You hadn't any strangers with you, I suppose?"

"Only two," Mr. Samuelson replied. "We were ten, altogether," he went on, counting upon his fingers - "and a very nice little party too. First of all my wife and myself. Then Mr. and Mrs. Max Solomon - Solomon, the great fruiterers in Covent Garden, you know; man worth a quarter of a million of money and a distant connection of my wife - very distant, worse luck! Then there was Mr. Sidney Hollingworth, a young man in my office; but he doesn't count, because he stayed on chatting with me about business after the others had gone, and he was with us when the theft was discovered. Then there was my wife's widowed sister, Mrs. Rosenthal. We can leave her out. That's six. Then there was Alderman Sir Henry Dabbs and his wife. You may know the name - large portmanteau manufacturers in Spitalfields and certain to be Lord Mayor before long. His wife was wearing jewelry herself last night worth, I should say, from twenty to twenty-five thousand pounds; so my wife's little bit wouldn't do them much good, eh?"

"It certainly doesn't seem like it," I admitted. "So far, your list of guests seems to have been entirely reputable."

"The only two left," Mr. Samuelson concluded, "are an American gentleman and his daughter, a Mr. and Miss Parker whom we met on the train coming up from Brighton - a very delightful gentleman and most popular he was with all of us. The young lady, too, was

　　　　E. Phillips Oppenheim

perfectly charming. To hear him talk I should have put him down myself as a man worth all the money he needed, and more; and the young lady had got that trick of wearing her clothes and talking as though she were born a princess. Real style, I should have said - both of them. Still, the fact remains that they came in a motor car with two men-servants; that it waited for them; and that this detective from Scotland Yard - Mr. Cullen, I think his name is - has fairly got his knife into them."

"And now," I remarked, smiling, "you are perhaps coming to the object of your visit to me?"

"Exactly!" Mr. Samuelson admitted. "The fact of it is that in the course of conversation your name was mentioned. I forget exactly how it cropped up, but it did crop up. Mr. Parker, it seems, has the privilege of your acquaintance - at any rate he claims it. Now if his claim is a just one, and if you can tell me Mr. Parker is a friend of yours - why, that ends the matter, so far as I am concerned. I am not going to have my guests worried and annoyed by detectives for the sake of a handful of jewels. I thank goodness I can afford to lose them, if they must be lost, and I can replace them this afternoon without feeling it. Now you know where we are, Mr. Walmsley. You understand exactly why I have come to see you, eh?"

I pressed another cigarette upon him and lit one myself.

"I do understand, Mr. Samuelson," I told him, "and I appreciate your visit very much indeed. I am exceedingly glad you came. Mr. Parker told you the truth. He is a gentleman for whom I have the utmost respect and esteem. I consider his daughter, too, one of the most charming young ladies I have ever met. I am planning to give a dinner party, within the course of the next few evenings, purposely to introduce them to some of my friends with whom they are as yet unacquainted; and I am hoping that almost immediately afterward they will be staying with my sister at her place down in Suffolk."

"With the Countess of Aynesley?" Mr. Samuelson said slowly.

"Certainly!" I agreed. "I am quite sure my sister will be as charmed with them as I and many other of my friends are."

Mr. Samuelson rose to his feet, brushed the cigarette ash from his trousers and took up his hat.

"Mr. Walmsley," he said, holding out his hand, "I am glad I came. You have treated me frankly and in a most gentlemanly manner. I can assure you I appreciate it. Not under any circumstances would I allow friends of yours to be irritated by the indiscriminate inquiries of detectives. The jewels can go hang, sir!"

He shook hands with me and permitted me to show him out, after which he marched down the corridor, humming gayly to himself, determined to have me understand that a trifling loss of two thousand pounds' worth of jewelry was in reality nothing. I stood for some time with my back to the fire, smoking thoughtfully. Then the telephone bell rang. My gloomier reflections were at once forgotten. It was Eve who spoke.

"Good morning, Mr. Walmsley!"

"Good morning, Miss Eve!" I replied.

"Are you very busy this morning?" she asked.

"Nothing in the world to do!" I answered promptly.

"Then please come round," she directed, ringing off almost at once.

I was there in ten minutes. The hall porter, who had not yet completed his morning toilet, conducted me upstairs. In the morning sunlight the whole appearance of the place seemed shabbier and dirtier than ever. Inside the sitting room, however, everything was different. My own flowers had apparently been supplemented by many others. Mr. Parker, as pink-and-white as usual, looking the very picture of content and good digestion, was smoking a large cigar and reading a newspaper. Eve was seated at the writing table, but she swung round at my entrance and held out both her hands.

"The flowers are lovely!" she murmured. "Do go and sit down - and talk to daddy while I finish this letter."

I shook hands with Mr. Parker. He laid down the newspaper and smiled at me.

"A pleasant dinner last night, I trust?" I inquired.

His eyes twinkled.

"Most humorous affair!" he declared. "I wouldn't have missed it for worlds."

"From a business point of view -" I began dryly.

Mr. Parker shook his head.

"Mr. Samuelson's jewels," he complained, "were like his wines, all sparkle and outside - no body to them. Two thousand pounds indeed! Why, we shall be lucky if we clear four hundred!" The man's coolness absolutely took me aback. For a moment I simply stared at him. "He'll be round to see you this morning, sometime, about my character," Mr. Parker proceeded.

"He has already paid me a visit," I said grimly. "He was round at ten o'clock this morning."

"You don't say!" Mr. Parker murmured.

He looked at me hopefully. His expression was like nothing else but the wistful smile of a fat boy expecting good news.

"Oh, of course I told him the usual thing!" I admitted. "I told him you were a close personal friend; a sort of amateur millionaire; a person of the highest respect- ability - everything you ought to be, in fact. He went away perfectly satisfied and determined to have nothing to do with the guest theory."

Mr. Parker patted me on the shoulder.

"My boy," he said, "I knew I could rely on you."

"I propose," I continued, elaborating upon the scheme that had come into my head on the way, "to do more than this for you. I am asking some friends to dine to- night whom I wish you and your daughter to meet.

You will then be able to refer to other reputable acquaintances in London besides myself."

Eve turned round in her chair to listen. Mr. Parker, whose first expression had been one of unfeigned delight, suddenly paused.

"My boy," he expostulated, "I don't want to take advantage of you. Do you think it's quite playing the game on your friends to introduce to them two people like ourselves? You know what it means."

"I know perfectly well," I agreed; "but, as some day or other I'm going to marry Eve, it seems to me the thing might as well be done."

They were both perfectly silent for several moments. They looked at each other. There were questions in his face - other things in hers. I strolled across to the window.

"If you'd like to talk it over," I suggested, "don't mind me. All the same I insist upon the party."

"It's uncommonly kind of you, sure!" Mr. Parker said thoughtfully. "The more I think it over, the more I feel impressed by it; but, do you know, there's something about the proposition I can't quite cotton to! Seems to me you've some little scheme of your own at the back of your head. You haven't got it in your mind, have you, that you're sort of putting us on our honor?"

"I have no ulterior motive at all," I declared mendaciously.

Eve rose to her feet and came across to me. She was

wearing a charming morning gown of some light blue material, with large buttons, tight-fitting, alluring; and there was a little quiver of her lips, a provocative gleam in her eyes, which I found perfectly maddening.

"I think we won't come, thank you," she decided.

"Why not?"

"You see," she explained, "I am rather afraid. We might get you into no end of trouble with some of your most particular friends. There are one or two people, you know, in London, especially among the Americans, who might say the unkindest things about us."

"No one, my dear Eve," I assured her stolidly, "shall say anything to me or to any one else about my future wife."

For a moment her expression was almost hopeless. She shook her head.

"I don't know what to do with him, daddy!" she exclaimed, turning toward her father in despair.

"I'm afraid you'll have to marry him if he goes on," Mr. Parker declared gloomily; "that is," he added, as though he had suddenly perceived a ray of hope about the matter, "unless we should by any chance get into trouble first."

"Meantime," I ventured, "we will dine at eight o'clock at the Milan."

Mr. Parker groaned.

"At the Milan!" he echoed. "Worse and worse! We shall be recognized for certain! There's a man lives there whom I did out of a hundred pounds - just a little variation of the confidence trick. Nothing he can get hold of, you understand; but he knows very well that I had him. Look here, Walmsley, be reasonable! Hadn't you better drop this chivalrous scheme of yours, young fellow?"

"The dinner is a fixture," I replied firmly. "Can I borrow Miss Eve, please? I want to take her for a motor ride."

"You cannot, sir," Mr. Parker told me. "Eve has a little business of her own - or, rather, mine - to attend to this morning."

"You are not going to let her run any more risks, are you?"

Mr. Parker frowned at me.

"Look here, young man," he said; "she is my daughter, remember! I am looking after her for the present. You leave that to me."

Eve touched me on the arm.

"Really, I am busy to-day," she assured me. "I have to do something for daddy this morning - something quite harmless; and this afternoon I have to go to my dressmaker's. We'll come at eight o'clock."

"We'll come on this condition," Mr. Parker suddenly determined: "My name is getting a little too well known, and it isn't my own, anyway. We'll come as

Mr. and Miss Bundercombe or not at all."

"Why on earth Bundercombe?" I demanded.

"For the reason I have just stated," Mr. Parker said obstinately. "Parker isn't my name at all; and, between you and me, I think I have made it a bit notorious. Now there is a Mr. Bundercombe and his daughter, who live out in a far-western State of America, who've never been out of their own country, and who are never likely to set foot on this side. She's a pretty little girl - just like Eve might be; and he's a big, handsome fellow - just like me. So we'll borrow their names if you don't mind."

"You can come without a name at all, so long as you come," was my final decision as I took my leave.

CHAPTER VI

THE PARTY AT THE MILAN

The dinner party, which I arranged for in the Milan restaurant, was, on the whole, a great success. My sister played hostess for me and confessed herself charmed with Eve, as indeed was every one else. Mr. Parker's stories kept his end of the table in continual bursts of merriment. One little incident, too, was in its way exceedingly satisfactory. Mr. And Mrs. Samuelson were being entertained by some friends close at hand, and they appeared very much gratified at the cordiality of our greeting. I talked with Mr. Samuelson during the evening, and I felt that, so far as he was concerned at any rate, not a shadow of suspicion remained in his mind as to my two guests.

We sat a long time over dinner. Eve was between a cousin of mine - who was a member of Parliament, a master of foxhounds, and in his way quite a distinguished person - and the old Earl of Enterdean, my godfather; and they were both of them obviously her abject slaves. No one seemed in the least inclined to move and it was nearly eleven o'clock before we passed into the private room I had engaged, where coffee and some bridge tables awaited us. We broke up there into little groups. I left Eve talking to my sister and was on my way to try to get near her father when the Countess of Enterdean, a perfectly charming old lady who had known me from boyhood, intercepted me.

"My dear Paul," she said, "I cannot thank you enough for having given us the opportunity of meeting these most delightful Americans, and I really must tell you this - I had meant to keep it a secret, but from you I cannot; I knew all the time that the name of Bundercombe was familiar to me, and suddenly it came over me like a flash! Directly I asked Mr. Bundercombe in what part of America his home was, of course it was all clear to me. What a small world it is! Do you know," she concluded impressively, "that it was just these two people, Mr. Bundercombe and his daughter, who were so amazingly kind to Reggie when he was out in the States on his way to Dicky's ranch!"

I was for a moment absolutely thunderstruck.

"Did you - er - remind Mr. Bundercombe of this?" I asked.

She shook her head. She had the pleased smile of a benevolent conspirator.

"I will tell you why I did not, Paul," she explained. "Reggie is in town - just for a few days. I have sent him a telephone message and he is wild with delight. He has only just arrived from Scotland; but I told him Mr. Bundercombe and his daughter were here, and he is rushing into his clothes as fast as he can and is coming round. It will be so delightful for him to meet them again, and I really must try to think myself what I can do to repay all their kindness to Reggie."

E. Phillips Oppenheim

I felt completely at my wit's end! I saw the whole of my little scheme, which up to now had proved so successful, threatened with instant destruction. Lady Enterdean passed on, probably to take some one else into her confidence. I crossed the room to the little group surrounding my friend, and as soon as I got near him I touched him on the shoulder.

"Just one word with you, Mr. Bundercombe," I begged.

The little circle of men let him through with reluctance. I passed my arm through his and led him out toward the foyer.

"You seem," I declared bitterly, "to have chosen the most unfortunate personality! I wish to goodness you had remained Mr. Parker! This infernal name of yours, Bundercombe, has got us into trouble."

"In what way?" he asked quickly.

"Lady Enterdean has just been to me," I told him. "She has a son who has been traveling in the States and who was wonderfully entertained by two people of the name of Bundercombe in the very place you told me to say you came from."

"Well, that goes all right!" Mr. Parker remarked complacently. "We're getting the credit for it."

"Precisely," I admitted. "The only trouble is that Lady Enterdean has just telephoned to her son to come down at once and renew his acquaintance with you and Eve."

Mr. Parker whistled softly. His face had become

a blank.

"My! We do seem to be up against it!" he confessed uneasily.

"The young man," I continued, "will be here in ten minutes - perhaps sooner - prepared to grasp you both by the hand and exchange reminiscences."

Mr. Parker shook out a white silk handkerchief from his pocket and mopped his forehead.

"Kind of warm out here!" he remarked. "I'll just have to talk to Eve for a minute or two."

He had no sooner left me than I found I was absolutely compelled to devote myself to one or two of my guests who wished to play bridge, and others of whom I had seen little at dinner time. I kept looking anxiously round and at last the blow fell! The door opened and Lord Reginald Sidley was announced. He looked eagerly round the room.

"Hope you don't mind my butting in, old chap!" he said as he shook hands with me. "The mater telephoned that old Bundercombe and his daughter were here, so I just rushed round as quick as I could. Regular bricks they were to me out West! I don't see them anywhere."

I glanced round the room. Just at that moment a waiter from the restaurant presented himself. He brought me a card upon a salver.

"The gentleman asked me to give you this, sir," he announced.

I picked it up. On the back of a plain visiting card were a few hasty words, scrawled in pencil:

"So sorry - but Eve is not feeling quite herself and begged me to take her home at once quietly. My respects and apologies to you and all your delightful guests."

I read it out and passed it to Reggie. His face fell.

"If that isn't a sell!" he exclaimed. "Fancy your knowing them! Isn't Miss Bundercombe a topper!"

"She is certainly one of the most charming young women I ever met in my life," I admitted.

"I am glad, at any rate," Lady Enterdean declared, "that they have found their way to London. I shall make a point of calling on them myself tomorrow. Now, Paul, you must go and play bridge. They are waiting for you. Don't bother about me - I'll amuse myself quite well strolling round and talking to my friends." I made up a rubber of bridge, chiefly with the idea of distracting my thoughts. Presently, while my partner was playing the hand, I rose and crossed the room to the sideboard for some cigarettes. I found Lady Enterdean peering about with her lorgnette fixed to her eyes, apparently searching for something.

"Lost anything, Lady Enterdean?" I asked.

"A most extraordinary thing has happened, my dear Paul!" she declared, resting her hand on the bosom of her gown. "I am perfectly certain it was there a quarter of an hour ago - my cameo brooch, you know, the one that old Sir Henry brought home from Italy."

"Too large to lose anyway," I remarked cheerfully as I joined in the search.

We pulled aside a table and I almost collided with one of my most distinguished guests - Sir Blaydon Harrison, K.C.B. Sir Blaydon also, with an eyeglass in his eye, was moving discontentedly backward and forward, kicking the carpet.

"Silly thing!" he observed as he glanced up for a moment. "That little diamond charm of mine has slipped off my fob. I saw it as we crossed the foyer from the restaurant."

"Why, what has happened to us all!" my sister joined in. "Look at me - I've lost my pendant! Paul, did you give us too much to drink, or what?"

I am not sure that this was not the most awful moment of my life! A cold shiver of fear suddenly seized me. I looked from one to the other, speechless. If appearances had gone for anything at that moment I must indeed have looked guilty.

"Most extraordinary!" I mumbled.

"Oh! the things will turn up all right, without a doubt," Lady Enterdean declared good-humoredly. "Could we have a couple of waiters in and search properly, Paul? My knees are a little too old for this stooping."

"If you'll please all wait a few minutes," I begged earnestly, "I'll go out and make inquiries. Sir Blaydon, take my place in that rubber of bridge - there's a good fellow. I'll have the restaurant searched too. Don't mind if I am away a few minutes."

E. Phillips Oppenheim

I hurried out. As soon as the door of the private room was closed I made for the entrance of the restaurant as fast as I could sprint. Without hat or coat I jumped into a taxi, and in less than ten minutes I was mounting the stairs of Number 17, Banton Street, with the hall porter blinking at me from his office. I scarcely went through the formality of knocking at the door. Mr. Parker and Eve were both standing at the table, their heads close together. At the sound of my footsteps and precipitate entrance Mr. Parker swung round. One hand was still behind him. Upon the table a white silk handkerchief was lying.

"My dear fellow!" he exclaimed. "My dear Walmsley! What has happened?"

I opened my lips and closed them again. It really seemed impossible to say anything! Mr. Parker's expression had never been so boyish, so earnest, and yet so wistful. Eve was quivering with some emotion the nature of which I could not at once divine. I felt very certain, however, that she had been remonstrating with her father.

"Don't keep us in suspense, my dear fellow!" Mr. Parker implored. "What has gone wrong? Eve and I were just - just talking over your delightful party."

"And looking over the spoils!" I said grimly.

I went a little farther into the room, Mr. Parker, with a sigh, abandoned his position. He unclosed the fingers of his hand and removed the silk handkerchief. I saw upon the table my aunt's brooch, my sister's pendant and Sir Blaydon Harrison's diamond pig. I said not a word. I looked at them and I looked at Mr. Parker. He smiled weakly and scratched his chin.

"I didn't do so badly," he essayed apologetically. "To tell you the truth, I really hadn't meant - "

"Never mind what you meant!" I interrupted. "Please give me those things back again at once!"

Eve dropped them into the handkerchief, twisted them up and passed them across to me.

"I told daddy it was rather a mean trick," she sighed; "but really, you know, no people ought to carry about their valuables like that! It was trying us a little too high, wasn't it? And dear Reggie - did he arrive?"

For the first time I was really angry with Eve.

"If you will allow me," I said, "I will pursue this conversation to-morrow morning."

I tore downstairs, jumped into the waiting taxi and returned to the Milan. I entered the private room with a grave face. Evidently I was only just in time. The rubber of bridge had been broken up and my guests were standing about in little groups talking. I closed the door behind me and held up my hand.

"Blanche," I announced - "Lady Enterdean - I am delighted to say I have recovered everything."

"My dear boy, how wonderfully clever of you!"

Lady Enterdean exclaimed. "How relieved I feel! Most satisfactory, I am sure."

She sat down promptly. There was a little murmur of voices. My guests gathered round me. I drew a long breath and continued on my mendacious career.

"I have been closeted with the manager," I explained. "It was one of the underwaiters - the little dark one who brought in the coffee. The temptation seems to have been too much for him. He confessed directly he was questioned. He has restored everything and I thought it best to have him simply turned off without any fuss. Here is your pig, Sir Blaydon; your pendant, Blanche; your brooch, Lady Enterdean. I am exceedingly sorry you should have had any anxiety - but all's well that ends well!" I wound up weakly.

Every one was talking cheerfully. The great topic now was one of ethics: Had I acted properly in not charging the waiter? Fortunately some one discovered a little later that it was twelve o'clock and my little party broke up.

CHAPTER VII

"ONE OF US"

I was not altogether surprised to receive, on the following morning before I had finished breakfast, a visit from Reggie.

"Cheero!" he said brightly as he seated himself in my easy-chair and tapped the end of one of my cigarettes upon the tablecloth. "I haven't been up so early for months, but I had to find you before you went out - about these Bundercombes."

"What about them?"

"I want their address, of course," Reggie continued. "The mater wants to call this afternoon and I'm all for seeing Miss Bundercombe again. Ripping girl, isn't she?"

"Then prepare yourself for a disappointment, my friend," I advised, glancing at the clock. "They left for Paris by the nine o'clock train this morning."

Reggie stared at me blankly.

"Gone already?"

I nodded and invented a little difficulty with my coffee pot.

"Theirs was only a flying visit," I explained. "I was lucky to get hold of them for my dinner."

"I'm hanged if I understand this!" Reggie remarked, looking at me suspiciously. "Why, I spent the best part of three weeks with them in that Godforsaken hole out West, and they were as keen as mustard on my taking them round London. How long have they been here?"

"Not long," I answered. "Sure you won't have some coffee?"

Reggie ignored the invitation.

"They've got my address and there are the directories," he continued. "The funny part of it is, too, that I heard from Mrs. Bundercombe a week or so ago, and she never said a word about any of them coming over."

"They seem to have made their minds up all of a sudden," I explained. "They spoke of it as quite a flying trip."

Reggie coughed and stared for a moment at the end of his boot.

"Can't understand it at all!" he repeated. "Devilish queer thing, anyway! I say, Paul, you're sure it's all right, I suppose?"

"All right? What do you mean?"

" Between you and me," he went on - "don't give it

away outside this room, you know - but there have been rumors going about concerning an American and his pretty daughter over here - regular wrong 'uns! They've been up to all sorts of tricks and only kept out of prison by a fluke."

"You're not associating these people, whoever they may be, with Mr. And Miss Bundercombe?" I asked sternly.

Reggie gazed once more at the point of his boot.

"The thing is," he remarked, "are your friends Mr. and Miss Bundercombe at all?"

"Don't talk rot!"

"It may be rot," Reggie admitted slowly, "or it may not. By the by, where did you meet them?"

"If you don't mind," I answered, "we won't discuss them any longer."

"At least," Reggie insisted, "will you tell me this: Where have they been staying in London? I shall go there and see whether they have left any address for letters to be forwarded."

"I shall tell you nothing," I decided. "As a matter of fact I am finding you rather a nuisance."

Reggie picked up his hat.

"There is something more in this," he said didactically, "than meets the eye!"

"Machiavellian!" I scoffed. "Be off, Reggie!"

I had tea with Eve that afternoon and broached the subject of Reggie's visit as delicately as I could.

"You remember Lord Reggie Sidley?" I asked.

"Lord Reggie what!" Eve exclaimed.

"Sidley," I repeated firmly. "He spent three weeks with you out at your home in Okata. His threatened arrival last night was the cause of your father's precipitate retreat, and yours."

"Oh, that young man!" Eve remarked airily. "Well, what about him?"

" He has been round to see me this morning," I told her - "wanted your address."

She sighed.

"London will be getting too hot for us soon!" she murmured. "Am I engaged to him or anything?"

"Eve," I said, "when are you going to let me announce our engagement?"

"Our what?" she demanded.

"Engagement," I repeated. "I have proposed to you two or three times. I will do it again if you like."

"Pray don't!" she begged. "You are not going to tell me, are you," she added, looking at me with wide-open eyes, "that I have accepted you?"

"You haven't refused me," I pointed out.

"If I haven't," she assured me, "it has been simply to save your feelings."

I gulped down a little rising storm of indignation.

"You must marry sometime. Eve," I said. "There isn't any one in America, is there?"

"There are a great many," she assured me. "It was to get away from them, as much as anything, that I came over with father on this business trip."

"Business trip!" I groaned.

"Oh! I dare say it all seems very disgraceful to any one like you - you who were born with plenty of money and have never been obliged to earn any, and have mixed with respectable people all your life!" she exclaimed. "All the same, let me tell you there are plenty of charming and delightful people going about the world earning their living by their wits - simply because they are forced to. There is more than one code of morals, you know."

I flatter myself that at this point I was tactful.

"My dear Eve," I reminded her, "you forget that I have joined the gang - I mean," I corrected myself hastily, "that I have offered to associate myself with you and your father in any of your enterprises. I am perfectly willing to give up anything in life you may consider too respectable. At the same time I must say there are limits so far as you are concerned."

She pouted a little.

"I hate being out of things," she said.

"No need for you to be, altogether!" I continued.

"Now if I could institute a real big affair in the shape of a bucketshop swindle, in which your father and I could play the principal parts and you become merely a subordinate, such as a typist or something - what about that, eh?"

"It doesn't sound very amusing for me," she objected. "How much should we make?"

"Thousands," I assured her, "if it were properly engineered."

"I think," she said reflectively, "that father would be very glad of a few thousands just now. He says the market over here, for such little trifles as we have come across, is very restricted."

I groaned under my breath. In imagination I could see Mr. Parker bartering with some shady individual for Lady Enterdean's cameo brooch! I reverted to our previous subject of conversation.

"Eve," I went on, "I hate to seem tedious - but the question of our engagement still hangs fire."

"You persistent person!" she sighed, "Tell me, if I married you would all those people we met last night be nice to me?"

"Of course they would," I assured her. "They are only

waiting for a word from you. I think they must have an idea already. I am not in the habit of giving dinner parties with a young lady as guest of honor."

She was thoughtful for a few moments, and her eyes lit up with reminiscent humor.

"Dear me!" she murmured. "If only they knew! They hadn't any suspicions, I suppose, about those - those little trifles?"

"None," I replied. "I put it all on to a waiter."

"How clever of you! You really do seem to be a most capable person - and so masterful! I begin to fear that some day you'll have your own way."

Her eyes laughed at me. There was something softly provocative in them - a new and kinder light. I bent over her and kissed her. She sat quite still.

"Mr. Walmsley!"

"It's usual among engaged couples," I pleaded.

"Is it!" she remarked coldly. "Doesn't the man, as a rule, wait to be quite sure he is engaged?"

"Not in this country," I declared: "I have heard that Americans are rather shy about that sort of thing. Englishmen - "

"Oh, bother Englishmen!" she exclaimed, stamping her foot. "I don't believe a word I've ever heard about them. I suppose now I shall have to marry you!"

"I don't see any way out of it," I agreed readily.

She held up her finger. The door was quietly opened. Mr. Parker entered.

He was followed by the most utterly objectionable and repulsive-looking person I have ever set eyes on in my life - a young man, thin, and of less than medium height, flashily dressed in cheap clothes, with patent boots and brilliant necktie. His cheeks were sallow; and his eyes, deeply inset, were closer together than any I have ever seen.

"My dear," Mr. Parker exclaimed, "let me present Mr. Moss - my daughter, sir; Mr. Walmsley - also one of us. I have been privileged," Mr. Parker continued, dropping his voice a little, "to watch Mr. Moss at work this afternoon; and I can assure you that a more consummate artist I have never seen - in Wall Street, at a racetrack meeting, or anywhere else."

Mr. Moss smiled deprecatingly and jerked his head sideways.

"The old un's pretty fly!" he remarked, as he laid his hat on the table.

"I am very glad to know Mr. Moss, of course," Eve said; "but I am not in the least in sympathy with the - er - branch of our industry he represents. You know, daddy, it's much too dangerous and not a bit remunerative."

"To a certain extent, my dear," her father admitted, "I am with you. Not all the way, though. One needs, of course, to discriminate. Personally I must admit that the nerve and actual genius required in finger manipulation have always attracted me."

Mr. Moss paused, with his glass halfway to his lips. He jerked his head in the direction of Mr. Parker.

"He is one for the gab, ain't he?" he remarked confidentially to me.

For the life of me, at that moment I could not tell whether to leave the room in a fit of angry disgust or to accept the ludicrous side of the situation and laugh. Fortunately for me, perhaps, I caught Eve's eye, in which there was more than the suspicion of a twinkle. I chose, therefore, the latter alternative. Mr. Moss watched us for a moment curiously.

"What might your line be, guvnor?" he asked as he set down his glass.

"Oh, anything that's going," I replied carelessly. "City work is rather my specialty."

"I know!" Mr. Moss exclaimed quickly. "Slap-up offices; thousands of letters a day full of postal orders; shutters up suddenly - and bunco! Fine appearance for the job!" he added admiringly.

Eve sat down and began to laugh softly to herself. She had a habit of laughing almost altogether with her eyes in a way that expressed more genuine enjoyment than anything I have ever realized. She rocked herself gently backward and forward. Mr. Moss looked at us both a little suspiciously.

" Seem to be missing the joke a bit - I do! "

he remarked.

Eve sat up and was instantly grave.

"It is your clear-sighted way of putting things," she explained softly. "You seem to understand people so thoroughly."

"I don't generally make no mistake about the number of beans in the game," Mr. Moss observed in a self-congratulatory tone. "I can tell a crook from a mug a bit quicker than most."

"I have suggested to Mr. Moss, my dear," Mr. Parker intervened, turning toward us with beaming face, "just a little early dinner - say, at Stephano's - just as we are, you know. Will this be agreeable to you?"

"Certainly!" Eve assented promptly.

"Mr. Moss will tell us some of his little adventures," Mr. Parker continued, with satisfaction. "Considering that he has had twelve years' continual work, I think you'll all agree with me that his is a wonderful record. He has been compelled to enter into a little involuntary - er - retirement only once during the whole of that time."

Mr. Moss looked a little puzzled.

"He means lagged, don't he?" he remarked, a light breaking in on him. "Only once in my life - and that for a trifling beano - a lady's bag and a couple of wipes. I tell you it's no joke nowadays, though. They do watch you! The profession ain't what it was."

"You will come with us, won't you, Mr. Walmsley?" Eve begged, turning to me.

"I shall be delighted," I answered, with strenuous mendacity. "Did you say Stephano's, or what do you think of one of these places closer at hand? I was told of a little restaurant in Soho the other day, where the cooking is remarkable."

"I'm all for Stephano's," Mr. Moss declared, grinning; "and the sooner the better. One of the neatest pieces of business I ever did in my life I brought off there in the old bar. To tell you the truth, I'm getting a bit peckish."

"There is no reason," Mr. Parker agreed, "why we should not dine at once. It is very nearly seven o'clock. What do you say?"

"Yoicks! Tally-ho, for the Strand!" Mr. Moss exclaimed, with spirit.

We started off - four in a taxi. It was Mr. Moss who, with florid politeness, handed Eve to her seat; and it was Mr. Moss who entertained us on the way with light conversation.

CHAPTER VIII

AT THE ALHAMBRA

Luigi's face, when he met the Parkers and myself at the entrance of the restaurant, was a study. His polite bow and smile of welcome seemed suddenly frozen on his face as his eyes fell upon Mr. Moss. Mr. Moss was still wearing his hat, which was a black bowler with a small brim, set at a jaunty angle a little on one side and affording a liberal view of his black curls underneath. His linen failed completely to stand the test of the clear, soft light of the restaurant, and one might have been excused for entertaining certain doubts with regard to the diamond pin in his mauve tie and the ring that flashed from his not overwhite hand as he tardily removed his headgear.

"Bit of all right - this place!" Mr. Moss remarked, handing his hat to Luigi. "Who'll have a short one with me before we feed?"

Luigi passed the hat from the tips of his fingers to a subordinate. He showed us a table quite silently, handed the menu over to a *maître d'hôtel* and promptly departed. Looking round a little nervously I could see him gazing at us from his sanctum over the top of the blind!

"Mr. Moss, I see, has American tastes," Mr. Parker declared. "He likes an *apéritif* before dinner. Leave it to me, please."

Mr. Parker ordered a somewhat extensive dinner. Throughout the meal we listened to a series of adventures in which the hero was always Mr. Moss. We heard of wonderful hauls and wonderful escapes; detectives outwitted - exploits that reminded me more of the motor bandits of Paris than of our own sober capital.

Mr. Parker's attention never flagged. Halfway through the meal Mr. Moss suddenly put down his knife and fork. He broke off in the middle of a fascinating narration of an episode during which he had ju-jutsued one detective, knocked another down, locked them both in an empty room, and strolled away with a cigar abstracted from the case of one of them and his pockets full of uncut emeralds. With his mouth open he was gazing fixedly across the room. There was a considerable change in his tone.

"'Ware 'tec'!" he said sharply.

We all looked in the direction he indicated, and we all recognized Mr. Cullen, who was apparently returning with interest our observation. I saw a grim smile upon his lips as he disappeared for a moment behind the menu card. For a man who had in his time treated detectives in such a cavalier way, Mr. Moss' change of color and subdued manner was a little extraordinary. He cheered up, however, after a little while.

"Our friend Cullen," Mr. Parker murmured, "seems to have taken quite a fancy to this restaurant."

E. Phillips Oppenheim

"Used to be on my lay," Mr. Moss remarked. "He's much too big a duke now for the street, though. They say he gets nearly all the high-class forgery and swindling cases."

"We have come into contact with him ourselves," Mr. Parker observed genially. "Seems to me there's a kind of want of snap about him compared with our American detectives; but I dare say he knows his business."

"Is your father really enjoying this?" I asked Eve.

"He absolutely loves it!" she replied.

I sighed.

"And I think," she added suddenly, "you are behaving beautifully - I almost love you for it."

I looked at her quickly and I felt rewarded for all I had gone through. Her attitude toward me was subtly different. Somehow I felt that I was being permitted a glimpse of the real Eve. Her eyes were soft; she patted my hand under the table. I could almost have shaken hands with Mr. Moss!

"What about a music hall afterward?" I proposed in the fullness of my heart. "Shall I send for stalls at the Alhambra?"

My proposal was received with unanimous approval. Our departure from the restaurant a few minutes later evoked almost as much comment as our arrival. Mr. Moss led the way, his hands in his trousers pockets and a large cigar, pointing toward the ceiling, protruding from the corner of his mouth. His slight uneasiness with regard to the whereabouts of his hat having been dispelled by its appearance before we finished our meal, he placed it on his head at its usual angle before we left the room.

Mr. Parker took his arm as they passed out, and I saw Mr. Cullen's eyes follow them from behind his newspaper. The two got into a taxi and Eve and I followed them in another, an arrangement that Mr. Moss appeared to regard with disfavor. Eve's hand stole into mine as we drove off.

"Do you know," she said seriously, "I think it's perfectly horrid to drag you about in such company! It's all very well for us, because we belong and we are in a strange city; but I saw some of your friends look at you and whisper. They must think you are mad!"

"So long as you are in it, dear," I assured her, "I don't care where I go or with whom."

"You don't look like that a bit, you know!" she sighed.

"As for the rest," I went on, "if you are really sorry for me - why, then, end it! Your father could spare us for a little time."

I could see she was becoming serious again. Lights flashed upon her face. I felt a sudden wave of pity mingled with my love for her. After all, there were times when her anxiety must have been almost insupportable.

"Eve, dearest," I whispered, "you must let me take you away from this. You must! You are too good and sweet ever to mix with these people - to live this life."

She half closed her eyes for a moment. When she looked at me again she was laughing.

"You're a dear boy!" she said. "Now help me out, please. We have arrived." We found four stalls reserved for us near the front at the music hall; and, after settling a slight preliminary difficulty, owing to Mr. Moss' reluctance to parting with his hat, we sat down to enjoy the performance. Mr. Moss seemed a little disappointed, too, that his bright and snappy order for drinks to the powdered official who showed us to our places was not at once executed; but otherwise he made himself very much at home.

We had been there perhaps half an hour when I saw a sudden change in his demeanor, which was almost at once reflected in the serious expression that had stolen into Mr. Parker's benign countenance. An old gentleman, white-haired, with rubicund face and a jovial air, had taken the seat next to them. He had the appearance of having come from the country and of having spent a happy day in town. Even from where I sat I could see protruding from his breast-pocket a brown leather pocketbook.

I watched them as though fascinated. The change in Mr. Moss was amazing. His reckless air of enjoyment had departed. He was still smoking, but he was all alert, like a cat ready to spring. Mr. Parker, too, was interested. I saw him whisper something in Mr. Moss' ear and I felt a cold foreboding of what was going to happen.

"I'm for a drink !" Mr. Moss declared in a rather loud

tone. "Come on, guv'nor!"

They both rose. The old gentleman drew in his legs to let them pass. Though I watched with fixed eyes I was absolutely unable to follow their movements, but when they had passed the old gentleman I could see from where I sat that his pocketbook was gone.

"Did you see that?" I whispered to Eve.

She shook her head.

"The old gentleman's pocketbook," I groaned; "they've got it!"

Eve for a moment sat quite still; she, too, seemed nervous. I was looking away again at the retreating figures of Mr. Parker and Mr. Moss. Suddenly my heart sank. I saw the old gentleman spring to his feet and hurry after them; and I saw, too, at the end of the line of stalls, Mr. Cullen and a companion standing, waiting. I rose quickly to my feet.

"I'm afraid there's going to be some trouble," I said to Eve. "Let me go and see if I can help. It looks as though the whole thing were a trap."

I followed quickly. It is only fair to Mr. Cullen to say that he conducted the affair with great discretion and with every consideration for the feelings of the management. He stopped Mr. Parker and Mr. Moss as they reached the end of the line of stalls.

"Please come with me," he said. "I have something to say to you outside."

Mr. Moss showed signs of an attempt to escape. He stooped for a minute as though to run, but a kick from Mr. Parker induced him to alter his mind.

"Wotcher want?" he asked belligerently.

The old gentleman had now reached them, red-faced and incoherent. He addressed himself to Mr. Cullen, and I no longer had any doubt whatever that the affair was a plant of the detective.

"I've been robbed of my pocketbook!" he exclaimed. "One of these two has got it - brushed up against me just now on the way out of the stalls. Where's the manager?"

Only a few people in the immediate vicinity were conscious that anything at all unusual was happening. The promenade just at that particular spot was almost deserted.

"This gentleman is certainly mistaken," Mr. Parker declared with dignity. "Neither my friend nor myself knows anything about his pocketbook."

"I am sorry," Mr. Cullen said politely, "but I shall have to trouble you to come with me to Bow Street at once - and you, too, sir," he added, addressing the old gentleman. "I am a police officer and we will go into the matter there. You will agree with me that it is well not to make a disturbance here. I have two assistants with me."

He indicated by a little gesture two men who had emerged from somewhere in the background.

"I will go with the utmost pleasure," Mr. Parker consented. "At the same time this gentleman has obviously been drinking and his charge is absurd."

It was precisely at this moment that I felt something hard pressed against my hand. With a dexterity that was nothing short of miraculous, Mr. Parker, who apparently was standing with his hands in his pockets, had suddenly forced one of them through some secret opening in his coat.

In those few seconds it seemed to me I lived a year. I had no time to think - no time to realize that if I failed nothing could save my appearance at Bow Street on the following morning as a common pickpocket. I gripped the pocketbook from his hand and, without changing a muscle, dropped it into the yawning overcoat pocket of the bucolic gentleman.

The moment was over and passed. Mr. Parker, with a movement forward, had covered my proceedings. I had been face to face with death years before, but I had never felt quite the same thrill.

"This way, gentlemen, if you please," Mr. Cullen directed softly.

"You will not object to my accompanying you?" I asked.

"Certainly not," Mr. Cullen replied; "I, in fact, am not sure that it would not be my duty to ask you to come."

"One moment!" I begged.

Mr. Cullen paused.

"The gentleman who made this charge," I went on, "seems to me to be in a very uncertain condition. Might I suggest that, before you commit yourself to taking these people to the police station, you just make sure he really has been robbed of his pocketbook?"

"Had it here," the old gentleman declared; "right in this pocket! Look for yourself - gone!"

"The old gentleman scarcely seems to me," I remarked, "to be in a fit condition to know which pocket it was in."

Mr. Cullen, who had been walking carefully between him and the other two, smiled in a superior way.

"Please feel in all your pockets," he told his accomplice.

The old gentleman obeyed. Suddenly he stopped short. A blank expression came into his face.

"What have you got there?" I asked.

He brought it out with ill-concealed reluctance. It was, without doubt, the pocketbook. I shall never forget Mr. Cullen's face! He was bereft of words. He stared at it as though he had seen it come up through the floor. Mr. Moss simply stood with his mouth open. Mr. Parker alone appeared unmoved by any emotion of surprise. His manner was serious - almost dignified.

"I want you to take this from me straight, Mr. Cullen," he said. "I am not a man who loses his temper easily, but you're trying us a bit high."

Mr. Cullen remained for a moment or two speechless. He looked at me and drew a long breath. I knew perfectly well what he was thinking. He had had a man on either side of Mr. Parker and Mr. Moss. The only person who could have transferred that pocketbook was myself. I could see him readjusting his ideas as to my moral character.

"Mr. Parker - gentlemen," he said, removing his hat, "pray accept my apologies. You are free to return to your seats whenever you choose. This gentleman was evidently mistaken," he added, speaking with withering sarcasm and turning sharply toward his coadjutor. "You oughtn't to come to these places in your present condition, sir. Take my advice and get along home at once."

The bucolic gentleman, who had completely lost his appearance of inebriety, mumbled a few incoherent words and departed. After his departure Mr. Parker assumed a more genial attitude.

"Well, well! I suppose you only did your duty, sir," he remarked, with a resigned sigh. "We were on our way to the bar. Will you join us, Mr. Cullen?"

I did not hear the detective's reply, but somehow or other we all drifted there. Mr. Moss at once found an easy-chair, which he pronounced to be "a bit of all right" and in which he assumed an easy and elegant attitude. Mr. Parker, Mr. Cullen, and I completed the circle, which now included a professional gutter-thief, a disappointed detective, Mr. Parker and myself. It was a unique moment in my life!

The wine affected the spirits of no one except, perhaps,

Mr. Moss; and him, when we finally broke up our party, we thought it advisable to get rid of in quick order. To my surprise Mr. Parker seemed in a particularly despondent frame of mind. He needed pressing even to come to supper.

"You were quick-witted, Walmsley," he admitted as we rolled away in the car, "quick-witted, I'll admit that; but you were dead clumsy with your fingers! I could see what you were doing from the back of my head."

"Really!" I murmured. "Well, I suppose that sort of thing is a gift. I only know that I hope I may never have to do it again."

Mr. Parker sighed.

"I fear," he said, "that your troubles with us will soon be over. Eve has been telling me about that young idiot of an Englishman who visited the Bundercombes out in Okata. If there was one man whose name I thought I was safe to make use of it was Joe Bundercombe!"

"It seems," I admitted, "to have been an unfortunate choice. What do you think of doing about it?"

Mr. Parker apparently had no immediate answer ready for me. During our brief ride in the motor and in the early stages of supper he was afflicted by a taciturnity that made him almost negligible as a companion. And then suddenly a light broke over his face. He had the appearance of a shipwrecked mariner who suddenly catches sight of land in the offing. His lips were a little parted, his boyish face all aglow.

" Walmsley , my dear fellow!" he exclaimed. "Eve,

dear! The problem is solved! Raise your glasses and drink with me. Here's farewell to Mr. Joseph H. Parker and Miss Parker. And a welcome to Mr. and Miss Bundercombe, of Okata!"

"That's all very well," I said; "but Reggie will be on your track."

Mr. Parker beamed on Eve and me.

"We shall see!" he declared didactically.

CHAPTER IX

THE EXPOSURE

The next morning at twelve o'clock I took a taxi-cab round to Banton Street. The hall porter, who was beginning to know me well, seemed a little surprised at my appearance.

"Is the young lady upstairs?" I asked.

He was distinctly taken aback.

"Mr. Parker and his daughter have gone," he told me. I stopped on my way to the stairs.

"Gone?" I repeated.

"Went off this morning," he continued; "two taxi-cabs full of luggage."

"Aren't they coming back?"

"No signs of it."

"Did they leave any address?"

"None!"

"Are you sure?" I persisted. "Please ask at the office."

The porter left me for a moment, but returned shaking his head.

"Mr. Parker said there would be no messages or letters, and accordingly he left no address."

I turned slowly away. The hall porter followed me. He was drawing something from his waistcoat pocket.

"I wouldn't do a thing," he declared, "to get Mr. Parker into any trouble - for a nicer, freer-handed gentleman never came inside the hotel; but I don't know as there's much harm in showing you this, being as you're a friend. I picked it up in the sitting room after they'd gone."

He held out a cablegram. Before I realized what I was doing, I had read it. It was handed in at New York:

"Look out! H - sailed last Saturday!"

"Pretty badly scared of H - he was!" the hall porter remarked. "Ten minutes after that cablegram came they were hard at it, packing."

I gave the man a tip and drove back to my rooms, where I spent a restless morning, then lunched at my club and returned to the Milan afterward, only in the hope that I might find there a note or a message. There was nothing, however. Just as I was starting to go out the telephone bell rang. I took up the receiver. It was Eve's voice.

"Is that Mr. Walmsley?"

"It is," I admitted. "How are you, Eve?"

"Quite well, thank you."

"Still in London?"

"Certainly. Would you like to come and have tea with me?"

"Rather!" I replied enthusiastically. "Where are you?"

"Hiding!"

"That's all right," I replied. "I shan't give it away. Where shall I find you?"

"Well," she said, "we talked it over and decided that the best hiding place was one of the larger hotels. We are at the Ritz."

"I'll come right along if I may."

"Very well," she agreed. "Ask for Mr. Bundercombe."

I groaned under my breath, but I made no further comment; and in a very few minutes I presented myself at the Ritz Hotel. I was escorted upstairs and ushered into a very delightful suite on the second floor. Eve rose to meet me from behind a little tea-table. She was charmingly dressed and looking exceedingly well. Mr. Bundercombe, on the other hand, who was walking up and down the apartment with his hands behind his back, was distinctly nervous. He nodded at my entrance.

"How are you, Walmsley?" he said. "How are you?"

"I am quite well, sir, thank you," I replied, a little stupefied.

"Say, I'm afraid we are making a great mistake here," he went on anxiously. "We've slipped a point too near to the wind this time."

"If you'll allow me to tell you exactly what I think," I ventured, "frankly I think you have made a mistake. There's that matter of Reggie Sidley. He was worrying me all yesterday morning to find out where you were, and when I evaded the point he told me straight that he didn't believe you were the Bundercombes at all. He is always in and out of this place, and if he sees your name on the register - or his mother, Lady Enterdean, sees it - it seems to me it's about all up!"

"A piece of bravado, I must admit," Mr. Parker muttered - "a piece of absolute bravado! But there's the young woman who's responsible!" he added, shaking his fist at Eve. "I may have suggested our coming to your party as the Bundercombes, but it was Eve's idea that we put up this little piece of bluff. Now I'm all for Paris!" he went on insinuatingly.

At that precise moment I felt that there was nothing I wanted so much as to get Eve away from the Ritz, and I fell in with the scheme.

"We'll all go," I suggested. "I haven't had a week in Paris for a long time."

Eve handed me my tea.

"Don't count me in!" she begged. "I never felt less inclined to move from anywhere. If being Eve

Bundercombe means living at the Ritz I think I'd rather go on. The life of an adventuress is, after all, just a little strenuous and I am tired of living on the thin edge of nothing."

"Perhaps, before you know where you are," Mr. Bundercombe remarked gloomily, "you'll be living on the thin edge of a little less than nothing!"

There was a knock at the door. We all looked at one another. A magnificent person with powdered hair, breeches and silk stockings presented himself.

"Lord Reginald Sidley!" he announced.

In walked Reggie. He was correctly attired for calling and he carried a most immaculate silk hat in his hand. I fully expected to see him drop it on the floor, but he did nothing of the sort. He laid it upon a small table, paused for one second to shake his fist at me, and advanced toward Eve with both hands outstretched.

"At last I have found you, then!" he exclaimed. "Miss Bundercombe! Well, I am glad to see you!"

"Hello, Reggie!" she answered sweetly. "What a time you've been looking us up."

He was taken aback.

"Well, I like that!" he gasped. "And - how are you, Mr. Bundercombe?"

"Glad to see you!" Mr. Bundercombe replied cheerlessly.

The meeting had taken place and I seemed to be the only person in the room who was suffering from any sort of shock. Reggie was still holding one of Eve's hands and was almost incoherent.

"Come, I like that! I like that!" he exclaimed. "A long time looking you up indeed! Why didn't you let me know you were here? There hasn't been a line from you or from your father. We couldn't believe it when we heard that you had been at the dinner the other evening. I was never so disappointed in my life!"

I gripped Mr. Bundercombe by the arm and led him firmly to one side.

"Look here," I said, "is your name Bundercombe?"

"It is," he admitted gloomily.

"Are you a millionaire?" I persisted.

"Multi!" he groaned.

"Then what the blazes - what the - "

I stopped short. Once more the door was opened - this time without the formality of a knock. If Mr. Bundercombe had seemed anxious and depressed before it was obvious now that the worst had happened. All the cheerful life seemed to have faded from his good-humored face. He had literally collapsed in his clothes. Even Eve gave a little shriek.

Upon the threshold stood Mr. Cullen, and by his side a lady who might have been anywhere between fifty and sixty years old. She was dressed in a particularly unattractive checked traveling suit, with a little satchel suspended from a shiny black leather band round her waist. She wore a small hat that was much too juvenile for her; and from the back of it a blue veil, which she had pushed on one side, hung nearly to the floor. Her complexion was very yellow; she had a square jaw; and through her spectacles her eyes glittered in a most unpleasant fashion. Her greeting was scarcely conciliatory.

"So I've got you at last, have I? Say, this is a pretty chase you've led me! Do you know I've had to desert my post as president of the Great Amalgamated Meeting of the Free Women of the West to come and look after you two? Do you know that three thousand women had to listen to a substitute last Thursday? - and after I'd spent two months getting my facts for them! Do you know that you're the laughing-stock of Okata?"

"No one asked you to come, mother," Eve remarked with a sigh.

"Asked me to come, indeed!" the newcomer retorted. "Look at you both! I've heard all about your doings. This gentleman by my side has told me a few things. I'll talk to you presently, young woman. But say, is there anywhere on the face of this earth such a miserable, addle-headed lunatic as that man whom it's my misfortune to call my husband?"

She shook her fist at Mr. Bundercombe, who seemed to have become still smaller. Then she looked at me, and at Reggie, who was standing with his mouth wide open. She fixed upon us as her audience.

"Look at him!" she went on, stretching out her hands. "There's a respectable American for you! For thirty years he works as a man should - for it's what a man's made for - and thanks to his wife's help and advice he prospers. Look at him, I ask you! A baby can see that he hasn't the brains of a chicken. Yet there he stands - Joseph H. Bundercombe, of Bundercombe's Reapers, with eight million dollars' worth of stock to his name!"

I saw Reggie's eyes go up to the ceiling and I knew he was dividing eight million dollars by five. An expression almost of reverence passed into his face as he achieved the result. We none of us felt the slightest inclination to interrupt. Mrs. Bundercombe's long, skinny forefinger drew a little nearer to her victim. Then she coughed - the short, dry cough of the professional speaker - and continued:

"Wouldn't you believe that was success enough for any reasonable mortal? Wouldn't you say that, with a wife holding an honored and great position in the State, and his daughter by his side, he'd settle down out there and live a respectable, decent life? Not he! First of all he wants to travel.

"What does he do, then, but take up what he calls a hobby! He buys and gloats over every silly detective story that was ever written; practises disguises and making himself up, as he calls it; takes lessons in conjuring; haunts the police courts; consorts with criminals - in short, behaves like a great overgrown child in his own native city, where the name of Bundercombe - from the feminine standpoint - realizes everything that stands for freedom and greatness. The time came when it was necessary for me to put down my foot once and for all. I called him to me.

E. Phillips Oppenheim

"'Joseph Henry Bundercombe,' I said,'there must be an end to this!' 'There shall be,' he promised. The next day he and Eve, my misguided stepdaughter, were on their way to Europe; and I am credibly informed they cheated a commercial traveler at cards on the way to New York. That I find him at liberty now, it seems to me, is entirely owing to the clemency and kindness of this gentleman, who recognized my description at Scotland Yard and brought me here."

"Say, all I'm prepared to admit about that is that it was somehow fortunate," Mr. Bundercombe remarked with a sudden revival of his old self, "that it fell to my lot to have Mr. Cullen investigate some of my small adventures!"

"Mr. Bundercombe," said Cullen severely, "I think you will do well to listen to your wife and to take her advice. There are one or two of these little affairs, you must remember, that are not entirely closed yet."

Mr. Bundercombe sighed. He adopted an attitude of resignation.

"Well, Cullen," he replied, "if my career of crime is really to come to an end I don't want to bear you any ill will. We'll just take a stroll downstairs and talk about it."

Mrs. Bundercombe, with a quick movement to the left, blocked the way.

"That means a visit to the bar!" she declared. "I know you, Mr. Bundercombe. You'll stay right here and listen to a little more of what I've got to say. Who this gentleman may be I don't at present know," she went on, turning suddenly upon me; "but I am agreeable to listen to his name if any one has the manners to mention it."

"Walmsley, madam," I told her quickly, "Paul Walmsley. I have the honor to be engaged to marry your stepdaughter."

Mrs. Bundercombe looked at me in stony silence. Twice she opened her lips, and I am quite sure that if words had come they would have been unkind ones. Twice apparently, however, her command of language seemed inadequate.

"So you're going to marry an Englishman," she said, glaring at Eve.

"I am going to marry Mr. Walmsley, mother," Eve agreed sweetly. "He has been such a kind friend to us during the last few days - and I rather fancy I shall like living on this side."

"Dear me! Dear me! I hadn't heard of this!" Mr. Bundercombe remarked with interest. "You and I will go downstairs and have a little chat about it, Mr. Walmsley."

He made another strategic movement toward the door, which was promptly and effectually frustrated by his wife.

"No, you don't!" Mrs. Bundercombe prohibited. "I've a good deal more to say yet. I haven't been dragged over the ocean three thousand miles to have you all slip away directly I arrive. A nice state of things indeed! My husband, Joseph H. Bundercombe, a suspect at

Scotland Yard, followed everywhere by detectives; and my daughter - "

"Stepdaughter, please," Eve interrupted.

"Stepdaughter then! - talking about marrying a man she's probably known about twenty-four hours and met at a bar or in a thieves' kitchen, or something of the sort! If you must marry an Englishman," she continued with rising voice, "why don't you marry Lord Reginald Sidley there? His father is an earl, anyway."

"His uncle's one," Reggie put in gloomily, jerking his head toward me. "Old Walmsley's all right."

Eve patted his hand.

"Good boy!" she said. "You know I never encouraged you - did I, Reggie?'"

"Encouraged me!" he protested. "I think, on the whole, you said the rudest things to me I ever heard in my life - from a girl, anyway. I imagine," he added, taking up his hat, "that it's up to me to leave this little domestic gathering."

"I'll see you out," Mr. Bundercombe declared with alacrity.

Mrs. Bundercombe, with her eyes steadily fixed upon her husband, stepped back until she blocked the doorway.

"My dear Hannah!"

"Your dear nothing!" she interrupted ruthlessly.

"You just sit down by the side of your daughter there and let me tell you both what I think of you and what I'm going to do about it."

"I think," I suggested, "a little taxi drive - Your mother and father no doubt have a great deal to say to one another, and you can receive your little lecture later."

Eve assented at once; and Mrs. Bundercombe, for some reason or other, only entered a faint protest against our departure. It was about five o'clock in the afternoon and the streets were crowded with every description of vehicle. The sun was still warm; there was a faint pink light in the sky - a perfume of lilac in the air from the window-boxes and flower-barrows. I took Eve's fingers in mine and held them. I think she knew that something in the nature of an inquisition was coming, for she sat very demure, her eyes fixed on the road ahead.

"Eve," I asked, "how about Mrs. Samuelson's jewels?"

"They were returned to her from 'a repentant criminal,'" Eve murmured.

"And the forged banknotes made by the young man in the Adelphi?"

"They were all destroyed as fast as father could buy them," she explained. "He has found the boy a post now with some printer in America."

"And the two thousand pounds at the gaming club - that first night?"

" Daddy made it three and sent it to a hospital. He

thought it would do them more good."

"You know, you're a shocking pair!" I said severely.

"Paul," she sighed, "you never can know how dull it was at Okata."

"I'm jolly glad it was!" I told her. "It gives me a better chance - doesn't it?"

"And we'll give daddy a good time whenever we can?" she pleaded.

"Always," I promised. "He's one of the best!"

"He's so clever, too!"

"Clever, without a doubt," I admitted, "only I think perhaps we might get him to use his talents in a more orthodox way. By the by," I added, putting my head out of the window, "I think it's getting a little chilly."

I ordered the taxi closed and we returned to the hotel. The hall porter drew me on one side confidentially.

"Mr. Bundercombe and the other gentleman, sir," he announced, "are waiting for you in the bar."

CHAPTER X

A BROKEN PARTNERSHIP

By what certainly seemed to be, at the time, a stroke of evil fortune, I invited Mrs. Bundercombe and Eve to lunch with me at Prince's restaurant a few days after our return from the country. Mrs. Bundercombe was graciously pleased to accept my invitation; but she did not think it necessary to alter in any way her usual style of dress for the occasion.

We sailed into Prince's, therefore - Eve charming in a lemon-colored foulard dress and a black toque; Mrs. Bundercombe in an Okata dressmaker's conception of a tailor-made gown in some hard, steel-ray material, and a hat whose imperfections were perhaps mercifully hidden by a veil, which, instead of providing a really reasonable excuse for its existence by concealing some portion of Mrs. Bundercombe's features, streamed down behind her nearly to her feet.

The *maître d'hôtel* who welcomed me and showed to our table found his little flow of small talk arrested by that first glimpse of our companion. He accepted my orders in a chastened manner, and I noticed his eyes straying every now and then, as though in fearsome fascination, to Mrs. Bundercombe, who was sitting very upright at the table, with her bony fingers

E. Phillips Oppenheim

stretched out and a good deal of gold showing in her teeth as she talked with Eve in a high nasal voice concerning the absurd food invariably offered in English restaurants.

Then suddenly her flow of language ceased - the bomb-shell fell! Mrs. Bundercombe's face became unlike anything I have ever seen or dreamed of. Even Eve's eyes were round and her expression dubious. I turned my head.

Some three tables away Mr. Bundercombe was lunching with a young lady - a stranger to us all She was not only a stranger to us all but, though she was remarkably good looking, there were indications that she scarcely belonged to our world.

All three of us remained silent for a moment. Then I coughed and took up the wine list.

"What should you like to drink, Mrs. Bundercombe?" I asked in attempted unconcern.

Mrs. Bundercombe adjusted her spectacles severely and transferred her regard to me. I felt somehow as though I were back at school and had been discovered in some ignominious escapade.

"You are aware, Paul," she replied, "that I drink nothing save a glass of hot water after my meal. The subject of drink does not interest me. I appeal to you now as a future member of the family: Fetch Mr. Bundercombe here!"

I shook my head.

"Mrs. Bundercombe," I said, leaning over the table, "your husband during his stay in London plunged freely into the Bohemian life of our city. I will answer for it that he did so simply in pursuance of that hobby of which we all know. I am convinced - "

"Paul," Mrs. Bundercombe interrupted, her voice if possible a little more nasal even than usual, "will you fetch Mr. Bundercombe here, or must I rise from my seat in a public place and remove him myself from - from that hussy?"

I appealed to Eve.

"Eve," I begged, "please reason with your stepmother. There are certain situations in life that can be faced in one way only. Mrs. Bundercombe will no doubt have a few words to say to her husband on his return. Let her keep them until then."

"Paul is right!" Eve declared. "Do take our advice!" she continued, turning to her stepmother. "Let us eat our luncheon quite calmly. I am perfectly certain dad will have some very good reason to give for his presence here with that young lady."

Mrs. Bundercombe rose to her feet. I hastened to follow her example. We stood confronting one another.

"It is either you or I, Paul!" she insisted.

"Then it had better be myself," I groaned.

I deposited my napkin on the table and made my way toward Mr. Bundercombe. I smiled pleasantly at him and bowed apologetically toward his companion.

"Sorry," I said under my breath, "but I am afraid Mrs. Bundercombe means to make trouble!"

Mr. Bundercombe looked at me with a gloriously blank expression. His manner was not without dignity.

"I regret to hear," he replied, "that any person by the name of Mrs. Bundercombe is looking for trouble. I scarcely see, however, how I am concerned in the matter. You have the advantage of me, sir!"

I stared at him and stooped a little lower.

"She's tearing mad!" I whispered. "You don't want a scene. Couldn't you make an excuse and slip away?"

Mr. Bundercombe frowned at me. He glanced at the young lady as though seeking for some explanation.

"Is this young gentleman known to you, Miss Blanche?" he inquired.

She set down her glass and shook her head.

"Never saw him before in my life!" she declared. "What's worrying him?"

"Hitherto," Mr. Bundercombe said, "my somewhat unusual personal appearance has kept me from an adventure of this sort, but I clearly understand that I am now being mistaken for some one else. Your references to a Mrs. Bundercombe, sir, are Greek to me. My name is Parker - Mr. Joseph H. Parker."

"Do you mean to keep this up?" I protested.

Mr. Bundercombe beckoned to the *maître d'hôtel* who came hastily to his side.

"Do you know this gentleman?" he asked.

The *maître d'hôtel* bowed.

"Certainly, sir," he answered, with a questioning glance toward me. "This is Mr. Walmsley."

"Then will you take Mr. Walmsley back to his place?" Mr. Bundercombe begged. "He persists in mistaking me for some one else. I am not complaining, mind," he added affably; "no complaint whatever! I am quite sure the young gentleman is genuinely mistaken and does not mean to be in any way offensive. Only my digestion is not what it should be and these little *contretemps* in the middle of luncheon are disturbing. Run away, sir, please!" he concluded, waving his hand toward me.

The *maître d'hôtel* looked at me and I looked at the *maître d'hôtel*. Then I glanced at Mr. Bundercombe, who remained quite unruffled. Finally I bowed slightly toward the young lady and returned to my place.

"Well?" Mrs. Bundercombe snapped.

"It seems," I said, "that we were mistaken. That isn't Mr. Bundercombe at all."

Mrs. Bundercombe's face was a study.

"Is this a jest?" she demanded severely.

" I wish it were , " I replied. " Anyhow , Mrs.

Bundercombe, you must really excuse me, but there is nothing more I can do. The gentleman whom I addressed insisted upon it that his name was Mr. Joseph H. Parker. No doubt he was right. These likenesses are sometimes very deceptive," I added feebly.

Mrs. Bundercombe rose to her feet. I made no effort to stop her; in fact her action filled me with pleasurable anticipations. She walked across to the table at which Mr. Bundercombe was seated. Eve and I both turned in our places to watch.

"Poor daddy!" Eve murmured under her breath. "Why couldn't he have chosen a smaller restaurant. He is going to catch it now!"

"I think I'll back your father," I observed. "He is quite at his best this morning."

The exact words that passed between Mr. Bundercombe and his wife we, alas! never knew. She turned her left shoulder pointedly toward the young woman, whom she had designated as a hussy, and talked steadily for about a minute and a half at Mr. Bundercombe. The history of what followed was reflected in that gentleman's expressive face. He appeared to listen, at first in amazement, afterward in annoyance, and finally in downright anger. When at last he spoke we heard the words distinctly.

"Madam," he said, "I don't know who you are, and I object to being addressed in a public place by ladies who are strangers to me. Be so good as to return to your seat. You are mistaking me for some one else. My name is Joseph H. Parker."

For a lady who had won renown upon the platform as a debater, Mrs. Bundercombe seemed afflicted with considerable difficulty in framing a suitable reply; and while she was still a little incoherent Mr. Bundercombe softly summoned the *maître d'hôtel*. It may have been my fancy, but I certainly thought I saw a sovereign slipped into the hand of the latter.

"Charles," Mr. Bundercombe confided, "my luncheon is being spoiled by people who mistake me for a gentleman who, I believe, does bear a singular resemblance to me. My name is Parker! This lady insists upon addressing me as Mr. Bundercombe. I do not wish to make a disturbance, but I insist upon it that you conduct this lady to her place and see that I am not disturbed any more."

The *maître d'hôtel's* attitude was unmistakable. Within the course of a few seconds Mrs. Bundercombe was restored to us. I thought it best to ignore the whole matter and plunged at once into a discussion of gastronomic matters. "I have ordered," I began, "some Maryland chicken."

"Then you can eat it!" Mrs. Bundercombe snapped. "Not a mouthful of food do I take in this place with that painted hussy sitting by Joseph's side a few feet away! Oh, I'll fix him when I get him home!"

She drew a little breath between her teeth, but she was as good as her word. She refused all food and sat with her arms folded, glaring across at Mr. Bundercombe's table. My admiration for that man of genius was never greater than on that day. So far from hurrying over his luncheon, he seemed inclined to prolong it.

There was no lack of conversation between him and his companion. They even lingered over their coffee and they were still at the table when Eve and I had finished and Mrs. Bundercombe was sipping the hot water, the only thing that passed her lips during the entire meal. I paid the bill and rose. Mrs. Bundercombe, after a moment's hesitation, followed us.

"Eve and I thought of going into the Academy for a few minutes," I said tentatively as we reached the entrance hall.

Mrs. Bundercombe plumped herself down on a high-backed chair within a yard of the door.

"I," she announced, "shall wait here for Joseph!"

I realized the futility of any attempt to dissuade her; so we left her there, spent an hour at the Academy and did a little shopping. On our way back an idea occurred to me. We reentered the restaurant. Mrs. Bundercombe was still sitting there in a corner of the hall.

"Thinks he can tire me out, perhaps!" she remarked in an explanatory manner. "Well, he just can't - that's all!"

I moved a few steps farther in and glanced down the restaurant. Then I returned.

"But, my dear Mrs. Bundercombe," I said, "your husband has gone long ago! He went out the other way. I am not sure - but I believe we saw him in Bond Street quite three quarters of an hour ago."

" There is another way out?" Mrs. Bundercombe asked hastily.

"Certainly there is," I told her; "into Jermyn Street."

"Why was I not told?" she demanded, rising unwillingly to her feet.

"Really," I assured her, "I didn't think of it."

She followed us out. We all walked down Piccadilly.

"Will you please," she said, "direct me to a tea-shop?"

I pointed one out to her. She left us without a word of farewell. Eve and I turned down into the Haymarket.

"Nice example your parents are setting us!" I remarked.

Eve sighed.

"I wish I knew what dad was up to!" she murmured.

At that moment we met him. He came strolling along, his silk hat a little on the back of his head, a cigar in his mouth, his hands grasping his cane behind his back. "Bundercombe or Parker?" I inquired as we came to a standstill on the pavement.

He grinned.

"Nasty business, that!" he remarked cheerfully. "Why don't you keep to the Ritz or the Berkeley? Anyway," he added, his tone changing, "I'm glad I met you, Paul. I want your help in a little matter."

I shook my head.

"Quite out of the question!" I declared emphatically.

"Don't forget that Paul is an M.P., dad!" Eve said severely. "You mustn't attempt to bring him into any of your little affairs."

"On this occasion," Mr. Bundercombe expostulated, "I am on the side of the law. Mr. Cullen, whom I am probably going to see presently, will be my brother-in-arms."

"What do you need me for, then?" I asked.

"As to absolutely needing you, perhaps I don't," Mr. Bundercombe admitted. "On the other hand, it's a very interesting little affair, and one in which you could take a hand without compromising yourself."

"What about Eve?" I inquired.

"Not this time!" Mr. Bundercombe replied. "The only risk there is about the affair," he explained, "is that it is just possible there may be a bit of a scrap."

"What's the program?" I asked.

"To-night, at home, at ten o'clock. Can you manage it?"

"Rather," I answered; "if Eve doesn't mind. This is the night you promised to go with your mother to a lecture somewhere, isn't it?" I reminded her.

She nodded.

"Very well," she consented resignedly, "so long as you

don't let him get hurt, dad."

"No fear of that!" Mr. Bundercombe declared cheerfully. "If they go for any one they'll go for me. So long, young people! At ten o'clock, Paul!"

At precisely the hour agreed upon that evening I presented myself at Mr. Bundercombe's house in Prince's Gardens. I noticed that the manner of the servant who admitted me was subdued and there was a peculiar gloom about the place. Very few lights were lit and the farther portion of the house, of which one could catch a glimpse from the little circular hall, seemed entirely deserted. I was shown at once into Mr. Bundercombe's study upon the ground floor. Mr. Bundercombe was seated at a writing table, with his face toward the door. He greeted me with a friendly nod and pointed to a little table upon which stood an abundant display of cigars and cigarettes of all brands.

I helped myself and lit a cigarette.

"May I know something of this evening's program?" I asked.

"Spoil the whole show?" Mr. Bundercombe objected earnestly. "Just play the part of assistant audience and stick this into your pocket, will you?"

He threw toward me a very small revolver that he had produced from a drawer.

"Only the last three chambers are loaded," he remarked. "You'll have to click three times if you do use it. I don't think you'll need to, though. Take a stall and watch the fun. I'll tell you only this: You remember Bone Stanley, as he was called in those days - the man who was sent to prison for fifteen years for bank robbery and for shooting the manager? Down Hammersmith way it was. The fellow was an American."

"I remember it quite well," I assented. "He was tried for murder and convicted of manslaughter."

Mr. Bundercombe nodded.

"He was released this afternoon. He'll be here in a few minutes."

"Here!" I exclaimed.

Mr. Bundercombe nodded but did not offer any further explanation. Coupled with a certain gravity of expression he had the appearance of a schoolboy for whom a feast was being set out. "Quite a pleasant little evening we are going to have!" he promised. "You wait!"

I frowned a little uneasily.

"You are quite sure you're not letting me in for - "

Mr. Bundercombe plunged into the middle of my little protest.

"You're all right, Paul!" he assured me. "Cullen's in the house at the present moment and there are two other detectives with him. They are letting me run this thing simply because I know more about it than they do; and for certain reasons I'm not giving my whole hand away. Don't you worry, Paul! You'll be all right this time. Listen!"

We heard a very feeble ring at the bell. Mr. Bundercombe nodded.

"That's Stanley," he whispered. "Sit down!"

A man was shown into the room a moment later. I leaned forward in my chair so as to see more distinctly the hero of one of the most famous cases that had ever been tried in a criminal court. Of his renowned good looks there was little left. He stood there, still tall, with high cheekbones, furtive eyes and long mouth. He wore good clothes, his linen was irreproachable, and he kept his gloves on. Nevertheless the stamp of the prison was upon him.

"Mr. Stanley?" Mr. Bundercombe said. "Good! I am glad you were prevailed upon to come."

"I am still wholly in the dark as to what this means!" the newcomer remarked.

"I'll tell you in a very few sentences," Mr. Bundercombe promised. "Will you sit down?"

"I prefer to stand," Stanley replied, "until I know exactly in whose house I am and what your interest in me is."

"Very well!" Mr. Bundercombe agreed. "Here is my history: My name is Joseph H. Bundercombe. I am an American manufacturer. I have made a fortune in manufacturing Bundercombe's Reaping Machines. You may call it a hobby, if you like, but I have always been interested in criminals and criminal methods - not the lowest type, but men who have pitted their brains against others and robbed them.

"As soon as I arrived in this country I found an interest in inquiring into the identities of American criminals imprisoned over here, with a view to helping any deserving cases. Your name came before me. I studied your case. I became interested in it. I learned that your time was almost up. A chance inquiry revealed to me a state of things that I determined to bring before your knowledge."

"You sent me a telegram," Mr. Stanley interrupted, "as I was stepping on the steamer at Southampton. I have returned to London for your explanation."

"You will probably," Mr. Bundercombe remarked genially, "be thankful all your life that you did. Now listen!"

"Who is this person?" Mr. Stanley asked, indicating me. "He is my prospective son-in-law, Mr. Paul Walmsley," Mr. Bundercombe explained; "a member of Parliament. I have asked him to be present because I may need a little support, and also because it may help to convince you that I am in earnest.

"Twenty years ago, Mr. Stanley, you came to the conclusion that honest methods were of little use to any one seeking to make a large fortune. You joined with two other men, Richard Densmore and Philip Harding, in a series of semicriminal conspiracies.

"You pooled all your money - you had the most - and you determined that if you could not make a living honestly you would rob those with less brains than yourself. When half your capital was gone, this Hammersmith bank robbery was planned and took place. You were the only one caught and you held your tongue like a man; but, all the same, you were used as a cat's-paw."

"In what way?" Stanley asked softly.

"You all three had revolvers; you all three arranged that they should be uncharged. Cartridges were put into yours without your knowledge. You held up your revolver and pressed the trigger, believing it to be empty. The others knew better. You shot the bank manager and in the stupefaction that followed you became an easy captive. The others escaped."

Stanley moved a little on his feet. His lips were slightly parted, his eyes fixed upon Mr. Bundercombe.

"What story is this you are telling me?" he muttered.

"A true one!" Mr. Bundercombe continued.

"Now listen! The total amount in possession of your two confederates when you went into prison was under a thousand pounds. You heard from them periodically as struggling paupers. Harding met you out of prison. He was almost in rags. They were at the end of their resources, he told you. He gave you a hundred pounds, to procure which, he assured you with tears in his eyes, they had almost beggared themselves. It was to enable you to leave the country and make a fresh start.

"You were even grateful. You shook him by the hand. You left him at the hotel at Southampton only an hour before you got my telegram."

"What of it?" Stanley asked.

"Nothing, except this," Mr. Bundercombe concluded: "Your two partners were so scared at the result of the Hammersmith affair and at your sentence that they turned over a new leaf. They went into business as outside stockbrokers - with your capital. The agreement as to a third profits was still in force. They had what I can describe only as the devil's own luck. I should say their total capital to-day is at least fifty thousand pounds.

"The time came for you to be released. They had no idea of parting with a third of their money and taking you into the business. All the time they had deceived you. They continued the deception. Harding met you as a poor man. But for me you would have been on your way to South Africa by this time, with a hundred pounds in your pocket."

"Is what you are telling me the truth?" Stanley demanded.

"Absolutely!" Mr. Bundercombe declared. "I stumbled across the truth in making inquiries concerning you and your probable future. I had meant, as a matter of fact, to put up a little money of my own to give you a fresh start. In the course of these inquiries I happened to run across a young woman who had been a typist in Harding's office. It was from her I learned the truth. As he rose in the world Harding seems to have treated the girl badly. A little kindness and a little attention on my part, and I learned the truth. She placed me in possession of the whole story after we had lunched together to-day."

Stanley at last took the chair he had so long refused. He sat with his arms folded.

"And I kept my mouth closed!" he muttered. "It was their job. I would no more have pulled the trigger of my revolver than I would have shot myself - if I had known. It was they who put the cartridges there!"

He sat for a moment quite still. Mr. Bundercombe rang the bell.

"The gentlemen I am expecting," he said, "will be here in a moment. You can show them in directly they arrive."

The man bowed and withdrew. Mr. Bundercombe turned to his visitor.

"I have made the acquaintance," he continued, "of these two men, your late partners - sought them out and made it purposely. They are coming here to see me to-night. They fancy that it is just a friendly call. They know that I have money to invest. I have even made use of them, employed them to buy for me bonds of my own choosing. They think it is an affair of a little business chat, perhaps, and a restaurant supper. Pull yourself together, Stanley! Go into that corner, behind the curtain. Wait your time!"

Stanley rose slowly to his feet. His face was drawn as though with pain.

"It isn't so much the money," he muttered, "only I thought - I fancied they would have been there to meet me, to shake me by the hand, to stay with me! And they wanted to push me off out of the country!"

He opened his lips a little wider and swore, softly but vindictively. Then the bell rang. Mr. Bundercombe hastened to push him out of sight. We heard the sound of strange voices in the hall. When the door was opened it was obvious that the whole house was lit up. From somewhere in the distance came the soft music of a piano.

Mr. Harding and Mr. Densmore were announced. I looked at them curiously. They were both most correctly dressed in evening clothes. They both had somehow the hard expression of worldly men, tempered not altogether pleasantly by symptoms of good living. They greeted Mr. Bundercombe with bluff heartiness. He gave them each a hand.

"Now, my friends," he said, "welcome to my house! Paul," he added, turning to me, "let me introduce my two friends, Mr. Harding and Mr. Densmore - Mr. Paul Walmsley. Mr. Walmsley has just been returned for the western division of Bedfordshire."

They greeted me with more than affability. Mr. Harding assured me he had read my speeches. Mr. Densmore thought no one was more to be envied than a man who had the gifts that secured for him a seat in Parliament.

"It's early yet," Mr. Bundercombe declared genially. "Let's sit down. Tell me a little about English business. It interests me. You bought those Chilean bonds all right, I see. They are up an eighth to-night."

"A good purchase, Mr. Bundercombe," Mr. Harding assured him; "a very good purchase! After all, though, there's not much money to be made out of those government things. Now we've a little affair of our own - what do you say, Densmore?" he broke off, looking toward his partner. "We could afford to let Mr. Bundercombe come in a little way with us, I think?"

Mr. Densmore nodded.

"Not more than five," he said warningly. "Remember what you promised the Rothschild people."

Mr. Harding nodded and crossed his knees. He lit a cigar from the box Mr. Bundercombe passed round.

"This sounds interesting!" the latter remarked. "I dare say Mr. Walmsley, too, has a little spare money for investment."

Mr. Densmore sighed, though his eyes were brightening.

"It's too good a thing," he explained confidentially, "to let the world into. Between ourselves, there's a fortune in it, and we want to keep it among our friends."

He drew a dummy prospectus from his vest pocket and began a long-winded recital of some figures in which I was not particularly interested. Mr. Bundercombe, however, appeared to be greatly impressed by what he heard.

"Gentlemen," he said, "there's just one little thing: American business methods and English are different in one respect. In my country we've got a sort of official guide that tells us exactly whom we are dealing with and what their means are. Now I know you are good fellows and it seems to me I'll be glad to go into this little affair with you; but we are strangers financially, aren't we? Now if you were Americans I should say to you: 'What's your rating?' and you'd tell me, because you'd know that I could look it up in a business guide in ten minutes."

"Perfectly sound," Mr. Harding admitted - "perfectly! Neither my partner nor I have anything to conceal. Last Christmas we were worth just over sixty thousand pounds and since then we've made a bit."

"You've no other partner?" Mr. Bundercombe inquired.

"Certainly not!" Mr. Harding replied.

"Then what about our friend Stanley?" Mr. Bundercombe asked quietly.

Almost as he spoke Stanley walked into the middle of the little group. I have never in the whole course of my life seen two men so thoroughly and entirely amazed. Mr. Harding dropped his cigar on the carpet, where he let it remain. They stared at Stanley as though they were looking upon a ghost. Both men seemed somehow to have lost their confident bearing - seemed to have shrunken into smaller, less assertive, meaner beings.

"Sixty thousand pounds," Mr. Bundercombe went on - "one-third of which belongs to Stanley here."

"Absurd!" Harding faltered.

"Nothing - nothing of the sort!" Densmore declared.

Mr. Bundercombe very carefully lit another cigar.

Then he rang the bell. Harding rose to his feet. He was not looking in the least like the sleek, opulent gentleman who had entered the room a few minutes before.

"What's that for?" he demanded, pointing to the bell.

The door was already opened. Mr. Bundercombe indicated the young lady who stood upon the threshold - the lady with whom he had been lunching that day at Prince's.

"I only wished to have the pleasure," Mr. Bundercombe explained, "of presenting you two gentlemen - Mr. Harding especially - to this young lady."

"Blanche!" Mr. Harding exclaimed.

Mr. Densmore muttered something under his breath.

"My dear Miss Blanche," said Mr. Bundercombe, moving toward the door, "I will not ask you to stay, as our interview is scarcely, perhaps, a pleasant one. I simply wished you to show yourself so that Mr. Harding and his friend might understand how useless certain denials on their part would be. My servant will now place you in a taxi; and if you will do me the honor of calling here at eleven o'clock tomorrow morning I think I can promise you a satisfactory termination to this little affair."

The girl patted him on the shoulder.

"That's all right, Bundy!" she declared. "I hope you'll take me out to lunch again! As for him," she added, her eyebrows coming together and looking toward

Harding, "perhaps he'll understand now how well it pays to be a liar!"

She turned round and left the room amid a stricken silence. Mr. Bundercombe came back to his place.

"Gentlemen," he said, "I will be brief with you. It has given me the utmost pleasure to arrange this little meeting on behalf of my friend, Mr. Stanley. In the room on the other side of the passage is waiting my lawyer, who will draw up a renewal of your partnership deed with Mr. Stanley upon terms that we can discuss amicably. In the room behind this is waiting a particular friend of mine - Mr. Cullen, a detective.

"Remember," Mr. Bundercombe added, his voice suddenly very stern and threatening, "that through all the years that man - your rightful partner - has been in prison, through all the agony of his trial, the humiliation of his sentence, the name of neither one of you has passed his lips! Is it your wish that the truth shall now be told?"

They shrank back. Harding was pale to the lips. Densmore was shivering.

"Very well, gentlemen," Mr. Bundercombe concluded. "If I send for the lawyer Mr. Cullen can go. If you choose Mr. Cullen the lawyer can go."

Mr. Harding moistened his lips with his tongue. "We will make an arrangement," he said. "We have been wrong. Now that I see you here, Stanley," he continued, looking up with the first show of courage either of them had exhibited, "I am ashamed! It was a dirty trick! Forget it! After you were lagged we decided to turn over a new leaf and be honest. We've been honest - inside the law, at any rate - and we've made money. Come and take your share of it and forgive!"

"We were brutes!" Densmore agreed.

They were both bending over Stanley. Somehow or other his hands stole out to them. Mr. Bundercombe and I strolled outside.

"You might tell Mr. Cullen that we shall not require him this evening," Mr. Bundercombe instructed the butler. "Bring a bottle of champagne, and tell the gentleman from Wymans & Wymans and his clerk that we shall be ready for them in ten minutes."

CHAPTER XI

MR. BUNDERCOMBE'S WINK

I scarcely recognized Mr. Cullen when he first accosted me in the courtyard of the Milan. At no time of distinguished appearance, a certain carelessness of dress and gait had brought him now almost on a level with the loafer in the street. His clothes needed brushing, he was unshaved, and he looked altogether very much in need of a bath and a new outfit.

"May I have a word with you, Mr. Walmsley?" he asked, standing in the middle of the pavement in front of me and blocking my progress toward the Strand.

I hesitated for a moment. His identity was only just then beginning to dawn upon me.

"Mr. Cullen!" I exclaimed.

"At your service, sir."

I turned round and led the way back into the court.

"This is not a professional visit, I trust?" I said as we passed into the smoke room.

"Not entirely, sir," Mr. Cullen admitted. "At the same

time - " He paused and looked out the window steadily for a moment, as though in search of inspiration.

"I trust," I began hastily, "that Mr. Bundercombe has not - "

"Precisely about him, sir, that I came to see you," Mr. Cullen interrupted. "I am bound to admit that a few weeks ago there was no man in the world I would have laid my hands on so readily. That day at the Ritz, however, changed my views completely. I feel," he added, with a dry smile, "that I got more than level with Mr. Bundercombe when I sent for his wife."

"So it was you who sent the cables that brought her over!" I remarked.

"But please remember, sir," he begged apologetically, "that I had never seen the lady. I sent the cables, confidently anticipating that she would disclaim all knowledge of Mr. Bundercombe. When she arrived, and I realized that she was actually his wife, I forgave him freely for all the small annoyances he had caused me: my visit to you this morning, in fact, is entirely in his interests."

"What has Mr. Bundercombe been up to now?" I asked nervously.

"Nothing serious - at any rate, that I know of," Mr. Cullen assured me. "For the last fortnight - ever since Mrs. Bundercombe's arrival, in fact - Mr. Bundercombe has somehow or other managed to keep away from all his old associates and out of any sort of mischief. Last night, however, I was out on duty - I haven't had time to go home and change my clothes yet - in a pretty bad part, shadowing one of the most dangerous swell mobsmen in Europe - a man you may have heard of, sir. He is commonly known as Dagger Rodwell."

I hastily disclaimed any acquaintance with the person in question.

"Tell me, though," I begged, "what this has to do with Mr. Bundercombe?"

"Just this," Mr. Cullen explained: "I ran my man to ground in a place where I wouldn't be seen except professionally - and with him was Mr. Bundercombe."

"They were not engaged," I asked quickly, "in any lawbreaking escapade at the time, I trust!"

Mr. Cullen shook his head reassuringly.

"Rodwell only goes in for the very big coups," he said. "Two or three in a lifetime, if he brought them off, would be enough for him. All the same there's something planning now and he's fairly got hold of Mr. Bundercombe. He's a smooth-tongued rascal - absolutely a gentleman to look at and speak to. What I want you to do, sir, if you're sufficiently interested, is to take Mr. Bundercombe away for a time."

"Interested!" I groaned. "He'll be my father-in-law in a couple of months."

"Then if you want him to attend the ceremony, sir," Mr. Cullen advised earnestly, "you'll get him out of London. He's restless. You may have noticed that yourself. He's spoiling for an adventure, and Dagger

Rodwell is just the man to make use of him and then leave him high and dry - the booby for us to save our bacon with. I don't wish any harm to Mr. Bundercombe, sir - and that's straight! Until the day I met Mrs. Bundercombe at Liverpool I am free to confess that I was feeling sore against him. To-day that's all wiped out. We had a pleasant little time at the Ritz that afternoon, and my opinion of the gentleman is that he's the right sort, I'm here to give you the office, sir, to get him away from London - and get him away quick. I may know a trifle more than I've told you, or I may not; but you'll take my advice if you want to escape trouble."

"I'll do what I can," I assured him a little blankly. "To tell you the truth I have been fearing something of this sort. During the last few days especially his daughter tells me he has been making all sorts of excuses to get away. I'll do what I can - and many thanks, Mr. Cullen. Let me offer you something."

Mr. Cullen declined anything except a cigar and went on his way. I called a taxi and drove round to the very delightful house the Bundercombes had taken in Prince's Gardens. I caught Mr. Bundercombe on the threshold. He would have hurried off, but I laid a detaining hand on his arm.

"Come back with me, if you please," I begged. "I have some news. I need to consult you all."

Mr. Bundercombe glanced at his watch. His manner was a little furtive. He was not dressed as usual - in frock coat, white waistcoat and silk hat, a costume that seemed to render more noticeable his great girth and smooth pink-and-white face - but in a blue serge, double-breasted suit, a bowler hat, and a style of neckgear a little reminiscent of the Bowery. Something in his very appearance seemed to me a confirmation of Mr. Cullen's warning. He looked at his watch and muttered something about an appointment.

"I promise not to keep you more than a very few minutes," I assured him. "Come along!"

I kept my arm on his and led him back into the house.

"Eve is in the morning room," he whispered. "Let's go in quietly and perhaps we shan't be heard."

We crossed the hall on tiptoe in the manner of conspirators. Before we could enter the room, however, our progress was arrested by a somewhat metallic cough. Mrs. Bundercombe, in a gray tweed coat and skirt of homely design, a black hat and black gloves, with a satchel in her hand, from which were protruding various forms of pamphlet literature, appeared suddenly on the threshold of the room she had insisted upon having allotted for her private use, and which she was pleased to call her study.

"Mr. Bundercombe!" she exclaimed portentously, taking no notice whatever of me.

"My dear?" he replied.

"May I ask the meaning of your leaving the house like a truant schoolboy at this hour of the morning, and in such garb!" demanded Mrs. Bundercombe, eying him severely through her pince-nez. "Is your memory failing you, Joseph Henry? Did you or did you not arrange to accompany me this morning to a meeting at the offices of the Women's Social Federation?"

"I fear I - er - I had forgotten the matter," Mr. Bundercombe stammered. "An affair of business - I was rung up on the telephone."

Mrs. Bundercombe stared at him. She said nothing; expression was sufficient. She turned to me.

"Eve is in the morning room, Mr. Walmsley," she said. "I presume your visit at this hour of the morning was intended for her."

"Precisely," I admitted. "I will go in and see her."

I opened the door and Mr. Bundercombe rather precipitately preceded me. If he had contemplated escape, however, he was doomed to disappointment. Mrs. Bundercombe followed us in. She reminded us of her presence by a hard cough as Eve saluted me in a somewhat light-hearted fashion.

"Mind, there's mother!" Eve whispered, with a little grimace. "Tell me why you have come so early, Paul. Are you going to take me out motoring all day? Or are you going to the dressmaker's with me? I really ought to have a chaperon of some sort, you know, and mother is much too busy making friends with the leaders of the Cause over here."

She made a face at me from behind a vase of flowers. Mrs. Bundercombe apparently thought it well to explain her position.

"I find it," she said, "absolutely incumbent upon me, while on a visit to this metropolis, to cultivate the acquaintance of the women of this country who are in sympathy with the great movement in the States with which I am associated. It is expected of me that I should make my presence over here known."

"Naturally," I agreed; "naturally, Mrs. Bundercombe. I see by the papers that you were speaking at a meeting last night. That reminds me," I went on, "that I really did come down this morning on rather an important matter, and perhaps it is as well that you are all here, as I should like your advice. I have received an invitation to stand for the division of the county in which I live."

They all looked puzzled.

"To stand for Parliament, I mean," I hastily explained to them. "It seems really rather a good opportunity - as, of course, I am fairly well known in the district, and the majority against us was only seventy or eighty at the last election."

"Say, that's interesting!" Mr. Bundercombe declared, putting down his hat, "I didn't know you were by way of being a professional man, though."

"I'm not," I replied. "You wouldn't call politics a profession exactly."

Mr. Bundercombe was more puzzled than ever. His hand caressed his chin in familiar fashion.

"Well, it's one way of making a living, isn't it?" he asked. "We call it a profession on our side."

"It isn't a way of making a living at all!" I assured him. "It costs one a great deal more than can be made out of it."

Mr. Bundercombe stopped scratching his chin.

Mrs. Bundercombe sat down opposite me and I was perfectly certain that she would presently have a few remarks to offer. Eve was looking delightfully interested.

"Say, I'm not quite sure I follow you," Mr. Bundercombe observed. "I am with you all right when you say that the direct pecuniary payment for being in Parliament doesn't amount to anything; but what's your pull worth, eh?"

"My what?" I inquired.

"Dash it all!" Mr. Bundercombe continued a little testily. "I only want to get at the common sense of the matter. You are thinking of trying for a seat in Parliament, and you say the four hundred a year you get for it is nothing. Well, of course, it's nothing. What I want to know is just what you get out of it indirectly? You get the handling of so much patronage, I suppose? What is it worth to you, and how much is there?"

I spent the next five minutes in an eloquent attempt to explain the difference between English and American politics. Mr. Bundercombe was partly convinced, but more than ever sure that he had found his way into a country of half-witted people. Eve, however, was much quicker at grasping the situation.

"I think it's perfectly delightful, Paul!" she declared. "I have read no end of stories of English electioneering, and they sound such fun! I want to come down and help. I have tons of new dresses - and I can read up all about politics going down on the train."

"That brings me," I went on, "to the real object of my visit. I want you and your father - I want you all," I added heroically - "to come down with me to Bedfordshire and help. You were coming anyway next week for a little time, you know. I want to carry you off at once."

Mrs. Bundercombe, who had been only waiting for her opportunity, broke in at this juncture.

"Young man," she said impressively; "Mr. Walmsley, before I consent to attend one of your meetings or to associate myself in any way with your cause, I must ask you one plain and simple question, and insist upon a plain and simple answer: What are your views as to Woman Suffrage?"

"The views of my party," I answered, with futile diplomacy.

"Enunciate as briefly as possible, but clearly, what the views of your party are," Mrs. Bundercombe bade me.

"I won't have him heckled!" Eve protested, coming over to my side.

I coughed.

"We are entirely in sympathy," I explained, "with the enfranchisement of women up to a certain point. We think that unmarried women who own property and pay taxes should have the vote."

"Rubbish!" Mrs. Bundercombe exclaimed firmly. "We want universal suffrage. We want men and women placed on exactly the same footing, politically and socially."

"That," I said, "I am afraid no political party would be prepared to grant at present."

"Then, save as an opponent, I can attend no political meetings in this country," Mrs. Bundercombe declared, rising to her feet with a fearsome air of finality.

I sighed.

"In that case," I confessed, "I am afraid it is useless for me to appeal to you for help. Perhaps you and your father - " I added, turning to Eve.

"Let them go down to you in the country by all means!" Mrs. Bundercombe interrupted. "For my part, though my visit to Europe was wholly undesired - was forced upon me, in fact, by dire circumstances," she added emphatically, glaring at Mr. Bundercombe - "since I am here I find so much work ready to my hand, so much appalling ignorance, so much prejudice, that I conceive it to be my duty to take up during my stay the work which presents itself here. I accordingly shall not leave London."

Mr. Bundercombe cheered up perceptibly at these words.

"I am rather busy myself," he said; "but perhaps a day or two - "

I thrust my arm through his.

"I rely upon you to help me canvass," I told him. "A lot is done by personal persuasion."

"Canvass!" Mr. Bundercombe repeated reflectively. "Say, just what do you mean by that?"

"It is very simple," I assured him. "You go and talk to the farmers and voters generally, and put a few plain issues before them - we'll post you up all right as to what to say. Then you wind up by asking for their votes and interest on my behalf."

"I do that - do I?" Mr. Bundercombe murmured. "Talk to them in a plain, straightforward way, eh?"

"That's it," I agreed. "A man with sound common sense like yourself could do me a lot of good."

Mr. Bundercombe was thoughtful, I am convinced that at that moment the germs of certain ideas which bore fruit a little later on were born in his mind. I saw him blink several times as he gazed up at the ceiling. I saw a faint smile gradually expand over his face. A premonition of trouble, even at that moment, forced itself on me.

"You'll have to be careful, you know," I explained, a little apprehensively. "You'll have to keep friends with the fellows all the time. They wouldn't appreciate practical jokes down there and the law as to bribery and corruption is very strict."

Mr. Bundercombe nodded solemnly.

"If I take the job on," he said, "you can trust me. It seems as though there might be something in it."

"You'll come down with me, then," I begged, "both of you? Come this afternoon! The dressmakers can follow you, Eve. It isn't far - an hour in the train and twenty minutes in the motor. We may have to picnic a little just to start with, but I know that the most important of the servants are there, ready and waiting."

"Pray do not let me stand in your way," Mrs. Bundercombe declared, rising. "My time will be fully occupied. I wish you good morning, Mr. Walmsley. I have an appointment at a quarter to twelve. You can let me know your final decision at luncheon-time."

She left the room. Mr. Bundercombe, Eve, and I exchanged glances.

"How far away did you say your place was, Paul?" Mr. Bundercombe asked.

"Right in the country," I told him - "takes you about an hour and a half to get there."

"I think we'll come," Mr. Bundercombe decided, looking absently out the window and watching his wife eloquently admonish a taxicab driver, who had driven up with a cigarette in his mouth. "Yes, I'm all for it!"

My little party at Walmsley Hall was in most respects a complete success. My sister was able to come and play hostess, and Eve was charmed with my house and its surroundings. Mr. Bundercombe, however, was a source of some little anxiety. On the first morning, when we were all preparing to go out, he drew me on one side.

"Paul," he said - he had, with some difficulty, got into

the way of calling me by my Christian name occasionally - "I want to get wise to this thing. Where does your political boss hang out?"

"We haven't such a person," I told him.

He seemed troubled. The more he inquired into our electioneering habits, the less he seemed to understand them.

"What's your platform, anyway?" he asked.

I handed him a copy of my election address, which he read carefully through, with a large cigar in the corner of his mouth. He handed it back to me with a somewhat depressed air.

"Seems to kind of lack grit," he remarked, a little doubtfully. "Why don't you go for the other side a bit more?"

"Look here!" I suggested, mindful that Eve was waiting for me. "You run down and have a chat with my agent. You'll find him just opposite the town hall in Bildborough. There's a car going down now."

"I'm on!" he agreed. "Anyway I must get to understand this business."

He departed presently and returned to luncheon with a distinctly crestfallen air. He beckoned me mysteriously into the library and laid his hand upon my shoulder in friendly fashion.

"Look here, Paul," he said, "is it too late to change your ticket?"

"Change my what?" I asked him.

"Change your platform - or whatever you call it! You're on the wrong horse, Paul, my boy. Even your own agent admits it - though I never mentioned your name at first or told him who I was. All the people round here with votes are farmers, agricultural laborers and small shopkeepers. Your platform's of no use to them."

"Well, that's what we've got to find out!" I protested. "Personally, I am convinced that it is."

"Now look here!" Mr. Bundercombe argued; "these chaps, though they seem stupid enough, are all out for themselves. They want to vote for what's going to make life easier for them. What's the good of sticking it into 'em about the Empire! Between you and me I don't think they care a fig for it. Then all this talk about military service - Gee! They ain't big enough for it! Disestablishment too - what do they care about that! You let me write your address for you. Promise 'em a land bill. Promise them the food on their tables at a bit less. Stick something in about a reduction in the price of beer. I've seen the other chap's address and it's a corker! Mostly lies, but thundering good ones. You let me touch yours up a bit."

"Where have you been?" I asked, a strange misgiving stealing into my mind. "Have you been talking to Mr. Ansell like this?"

"Ansell? No! Who's he?" Mr. Bundercombe inquired.

"My agent."

Mr. Bundercombe shook his head.

"Chap I palled up with was called Harrison."

I groaned.

"You've been to the other fellow's agent," I told him; "the agent for the Radical candidate."

Mr. Bundercombe whistled.

"You don't say!" he murmured. "Well, I'll tell you what it is, Paul, there are no flies on that chap! He's a real nippy little worker - that's what he is! If you take my advice," he went on persuasively, "you'll swap. We'll make it worth his while to come over. I've seen your Mr. Ansell - if that's his name. I saw the name on a brass plate and I saw him come out of his office - stiff, starched sort of chap, with a thin face and gray side whiskers!"

"That's the man," I admitted. "He and his father before him, and his grandfather, have been solicitors to my people for I don't know how many years!"

"He looked it!" Mr. Bundercombe declared. "A withered old skunk, if ever there was one! You want a live man to see you through this, Paul. You let me go down and sound Harrison this afternoon. No reason that I can see why we shouldn't use this fellow's address, too, if we can make terms with him."

"Look here!" I said. "Politics over on this side don't admit of such violent changes. My address is in the printer's hands and I've got to stick to it; and Ansell will have to be my agent whatever happens. It isn't all talk that wins these elections. The Walmsleys are well known in the county and we've done a bit for the country during the last hundred years. This other fellow - Horrocks, his name is - has never been near the place before. I grant you he's going to promise a lot of very interesting things, but that's been going on just a little too long. The people have had enough of that sort of thing. I think you'll find they'll put more trust in the little we can promise than in that rigmarole of Harrison's."

Mr. Bundercombe shook his head doubtfully.

"Well," he sighed, "I'm only on the outside edge of this thing yet. I must give it another morning."

We had a pleasant luncheon party, at which Mr. Bundercombe was introduced to some of my supporters, with whom - as he usually did with every one - he soon made himself popular. Eve and I then made our first little effort at canvassing. Eve's methods differed from her father's.

"I am so sorry," she said as she shook hands with a very influential but very doubtful voter of the farmer class, "but I don't know anything about English politics; so I can't talk to you about it as I'd like to. But you know I am going to marry Mr. Walmsley and come to live here, and it would be so nice to feel that all my friends had voted for him. If you have a few minutes to spare, Mr. Brown, would you please tell me just where you don't agree with Paul? I should so much like to hear, because he tells me that if once you were on his side he would feel almost comfortable."

Mr. Brown, who had always met my advances with a

grim taciturnity that made conversation exceedingly difficult, proceeded to dissertate upon one or two of the vexed questions of the day. I ventured to put in a few words now and then, and after a time he invited us in to tea. When we left he was more gracious than I had ever known him to be.

"And you must vote for Mr. Walmsley!" Eve declared at the end of her little speech of thanks, "because I want so much to have you come and take tea with me on the Terrace at the House of Commons - and I can't unless Paul is a member, can I?"

"Bribery and corruption!" Mr. Brown laughed. "However, we'll see. Certainly I have been very much pleased to hear Mr. Walmsley's views upon several matters. When did you say the village meeting was, Mr. Walmsley?"

"Thursday night," I replied.

"Well, I'll come," he promised.

"You'll take the chair?" I begged. "Nothing could do me more good than that; and I feel sure, if you look at things - " I was going to be very eloquent, but Eve interrupted me.

"Let me sit next to you, please," she said, looking up at him with her large, unusually innocent eyes.

"Oh, well - if you like!" Mr. Brown assented.

We drove off down the avenue in complete silence. When we had turned the corner Eve gave a little sigh.

"Paul," she declared, "I don't think there's anything I've ever come across in my life that's half so much fun as electioneering! Please take me to the next most difficult."

If Eve was a success, however, Mr. Bundercombe was to turn out a great disappointment. He came home a little later for dinner, looking very gloomy.

"Paul," he said, as we met for a moment in the smoking room, "Paul, I've sad news for you."

"I am sorry to hear it," I replied.

"I've looked into this little matter of politics," he continued; "I've looked into it as thoroughly as I can and I can't support you. You're on the wrong side, my boy! I've shaken hands with Mr. Horrocks, and that's the man who'll get the votes in this constituency. I've promised to do what I can to help him."

I was a little taken aback.

"You're not in earnest!" I exclaimed.

"Dead earnest!" Mr. Bundercombe regretted.

"The chap's convinced me. I feel it's up to me to lend him a hand."

"But surely," I expostulated, "even if you cannot see your way clear to help me, there's no need for you to go over to the enemy like this! You're not obliged to interfere in the election at all, are you?"

Mr. Bundercombe sighed.

"Matter of principle with me!" he explained. "I must be doing something. I can't canvass for you. I'll have to look round a bit for the other chap."

"I really don't see," I began, just a little annoyed, "why you should feel called upon to interfere in an English election at all, unless it is to help a friend."

Mr. Bundercombe looked at me and solemnly winked!

"Say, that's the dinner gong!" he announced cheerfully. "Let's be getting in."

"But I don't quite understand - "

Mr. Bundercombe repeated the wink upon a smaller scale. I followed him into the drawing-room, still in the dark as to his exact political position.

The movements of my prospective father-in-law were, for the next few days, wrapped in a certain mystery. He arrived home one evening, however, in a state of extreme indignation. As usual when anything had happened to upset him he came to look for me in the library.

"My boy," he said, "of all the God-forsaken, out-of-the-world, benighted holes, this Bildborough of yours absolutely takes the cake! For sheer ignorance - for sheer, thick-headed, bumptious, arrogant ignorance – give me your farmers!"

"What's wrong?" I asked him.

"Wrong? Listen!" he exclaimed, almost dramatically. "In this district - in this whole district, mind - there is not a single farmer who has heard of Bundercombe's Reapers!"

"I farm a bit myself," I reminded him, "and I had never heard of them."

Mr. Bundercombe went to the sideboard and mixed himself a cocktail with great care.

"Bundercombe's Reapers," he said, as soon as he had disposed of it, "are the only reapers used by live farmers in the United States of America, Canada, Australia, or any other country worth a cent!"

"That seems to hit us pretty hard," I remarked. "Have you got an agent over here?"

"Sure!" Mr. Bundercombe replied. "I don't follow the sales now, so I can't tell you what he's doing; but we've an agent here - and any country that doesn't buy Bundercombe's Reapers is off the line as regards agriculture!"

"What are you going to do about it?" I asked.

"Do!" Mr. Bundercombe toyed with his wine glass for a moment and then set it down. "What I have done," he announced, "is this: I have wired to my agent. I have ordered him to ship half a dozen machines - if necessary on a special train - and I am going to give an exhibition on some land I have hired, over by Little Bildborough, the day after tomorrow."

"That's the day of the election!" I exclaimed.

" You couldn't put it off, I suppose? " he suggested.

"That's the day I've fixed for my exhibition at any rate. I am giving the farmers a free lunch - slap-up affair it's going to be, I can tell you!"

"I am afraid," I answered, with a wholly wasted sarcasm, "that the affair has gone too far now for us to consider an alteration in the date."

"Well, well! We must try not to clash," Mr. Bundercombe said magnanimously. "How long does the voting go on?"

"From eight until eight," I told him.

Mr. Bundercombe was thoughtful.

"It's a long time to hold them!" he murmured.

"To hold whom?" I demanded.

Mr. Bundercombe started slightly.

"Nothing! Nothing! By the by, do you know a chap called Jonas - Henry Jonas, of Milton Farm?"

"I should think I do!" I groaned. "He's the backbone of the Opposition, the best speaker they've got and the most popular man."

Mr. Bundercombe smiled sweetly.

"Is that so!" he observed. "Well, well! He is a very intelligent man. I trust I'll be able to persuade him that any reaper he may be using at the present moment is a jay compared to Bundercombe's - this season's model!"

"I trust you may," I answered, a trifle tartly. "I am glad you're likely to do a little business; but you won't mind, my reminding you - will you? - that you really came down here to give me a leg up with my election, and not to sell your machines or to spend half your time in the enemy's camp!"

Mr. Bundercombe smiled. It was a curious smile, which seemed somehow to lose itself in his face. Then the dinner gong sounded and he winked at me slowly. Again I was conscious of some slight uneasiness. It began to dawn upon me that there was a scheme somewhere hatching; that Mr. Bundercombe's activity in the camp of the enemy might perhaps have an unsuspected significance. I talked to Eve about this after dinner; but she reassured me.

"Father talks of nothing but his reaping machines," she declared. "Besides, I am quite sure he would do nothing indiscreet. Only yesterday I found him studying a copy of the act referring to bribery and corruption. Dad's pretty smart, you know!"

"I do know that," I admitted. "I wish I knew what he was up to, though."

The next day was the last before the election. The little market of Bildborough was in a state of considerable excitement. Several open-air meetings were held toward evening. Eve and I, returning from a motor tour of the constituency, called at the office of my agent. We chatted with Mr. Ansell for a little while and then he pointed across the square.

"There's an American there," he said, "that the other side seems to have got hold of. He's their most popular

E. Phillips Oppenheim

speaker by a long way; but I gather they're a little uneasy about him. Didn't I have the pleasure of meeting him at your house?"

"Mr. Bundercombe!" I sighed. "He came down here to help me!"

Mr. Ansell put on his hat and beckoned mysteriously.

"Come out by the back way," he invited. "We shall hear him. He is going to speak from the little platform there."

By crossing a hotel yard, a fragment of kitchen garden and a bowling green, we were able to come within a few yards of where Mr. Bundercombe, with several other of Mr. Horrocks' supporters, was standing upon a small raised platform. Two local tradesmen and one helper from London addressed a few remarks of the usual sort to an apathetic audience, which was rapidly increasing in size. It was only when Mr. Bundercombe rose to his feet that the slightest sign of enthusiasm manifested itself. Eve looked at me with a pleased smile.

"Just look at all of them," she whispered, "how they are hurrying to hear dad speak!"

"That's all very well," I grumbled; "but he ought to be doing this for me."

Her fingers pressed my arm.

"Listen!" she said.

Mr. Bundercombe's style was breezy and his jokes

were frequent. He stood in an easy attitude and spoke with remarkable fluency. His first few remarks, which were mainly humorous, were cheered to the echo. The crowd was increasing all the time. Presently he took them into his confidence.

"When I came down here a few days ago," we heard him say, "I came meaning to support my friend, Mr. Walmsley." (Groans and cheers.) "That's all right, boys!" Mr. Bundercombe continued, "there's nothing the matter with Mr. Walmsley; but I come from a country where there's a bit more kick about politics, and I pretty soon made up my mind that the kick wasn't on the side my young friend belongs to.

"Now just listen to this: As one business man to another, I tell you that I asked Mr. Walmsley, the first night I was here: 'What are you getting out of this? Why are you going into Parliament?' He didn't seem to understand. He pleaded guilty to a four-hundred-a-year fee, but told me at the same time that it cost him a great deal more than that in extra charities. I asked him what pull he got through being in Parliament and how many of his friends he could find places for. All he could do was to smile and tell me that I didn't understand the way things were done in this country. He wanted to make me believe that he was anxious to sit in Parliament there and work day after day just for the honor and glory of it, or because he thought it was his duty.

"You know I'm an American business man, and that didn't cut any ice with me; so I dropped in and had a chat with Mr. Horrocks. I soon came to the conclusion that the candidate I'm here to support to-night is the man who comes a bit nearer to our idea of practical politics over on the other side of the pond. Mr. Horrocks doesn't make any bones about it. He wants that four hundred a year; in fact he needs it!" (Ironical cheers.) "He wants to call himself M.P. because when he goes out to lecture on Socialism he'll get a ten-guinea fee instead of five, on account of those two letters after his name.

"Furthermore his is the party that understands what I call practical politics. Every job that's going is given to their friends; and if there aren't enough jobs to go round, why, they get one of their statesmen to frame a bill - what you call your Insurance Bill is one of them, I believe - in which there are several hundred offices that need filling. And there you are!"

Mr. Ansell and I exchanged glances. The enthusiasm that had greeted Mr. Bundercombe's efforts was giving place now to murmurs and more ironical cheers. One of his coadjutors on the platform leaned over and whispered in Mr. Bundercombe's ear. Mr. Bunder-combe nodded.

"Gentlemen," he concluded, "I'm told that my time is up. I have explained my views to you and told you why I think you ought to vote for Mr. Horrocks. I've nothing to say against the other fellow, except that I don't understand his point of view. Mr. Horrocks I do understand. He's out to do himself a bit o'good and it's up to you to help him."

A determined tug at Mr. Bundercombe's coattails by one of the men on the platform brought him to his seat amid loud bursts of laughter and more cheers. Eve gripped my arm and we turned slowly away.

"It's a privilege," I declared solemnly, "to have ever known your father! If I only had an idea what he meant about those reaping machines! You couldn't give me a hint, I suppose, Eve?" She shook her head.

"Better wait!"

In the excitement of that final day I think both Eve and I completely forgot all about Mr. Bundercombe. It was not until we were on our way back from a motor tour through the outlying parts of the district that we were forcibly reminded of his existence. Quite close to Little Bildborough, the only absolutely hostile part of my constituency, we came upon what was really an extraordinary sight. Our chauffeur of his own accord drew up by the side of the road. Eve and I rose in our places.

In a large field on our left was gathered together apparently the whole population of the district. In one corner was a huge marquee, through the open flaps of which we could catch a glimpse of a sumptuously arranged cold collation. On a long table just outside, covered with a white cloth, was a vast array of bottles and beside it stood a man in a short linen jacket, who struck me as being suspiciously like Fritz, the bartender at one of Mr. Bundercombe's favorite haunts in London.

Toward the center of the field, seated upon a ridiculously inadequate seat on the top of a reaping machine, was Mr. Bundercombe. He had divested himself of coat and waistcoat, and was hatless. The perspiration was streaming down his face as he gripped the steering wheel. He was followed by a little crowd of children and sympathizing men, who cheered him

E. Phillips Oppenheim

all the time.

At a little distance away, on the other side of a red flag, Henry Jonas, the large farmer of the district, and the speaker on whom my opponent chiefly relied, was seated upon a similar machine in a similar state of undress. It was apparent, however, even to us, that Mr. Bundercombe's progress was at least twice as rapid as his opponent's.

"What on earth is it all about?" I exclaimed, absolutely bewildered.

Eve, who was standing by my side, clasped her hands round my arm.

"It seems to me," she murmured sweetly, "as if dad were trying his reaping machine against some one else's."

I looked at her demure little smile and I looked at the field in which I recognized very many of my staunchest opponents. Then I looked at the marquee. The table there must have been set for at least a hundred people. Suddenly I received a shock. Seated underneath the hedge, hatless and coatless, with his hair in picturesque disorder, was Mr. Jonas' cousin, also a violent opponent of my politics, and a nonconformist. He had a huge tumbler by his side, which - seeing me - he raised to his lips.

"Good old Walmsley!" he shouted out. "No politics today! Much too hot! Come in and see the reaping match."

He took a long drink and I sat down in the car.

"You know," I said to Mr. Ansell, who was standing on the front seat, "there'll be trouble about this!"

Mr. Ansell was looking a little grave himself.

"Is Mr. Bundercombe really the manufacturer of that machine?" he asked.

"Of course he is!" Eve replied. "It's the one hobby of his life - or, rather, it used to be," she corrected herself hastily. "Even now, when he begins talking about his reaping machine he forgets everything else."

Mr. Ansell hurried away and made a few inquiries. Meanwhile we watched the progress of the match. Every time Mr. Bundercombe had to turn he rocked in his seat and retained his balance only with difficulty. At every successful effort he was loudly cheered by a little group of following enthusiasts. Mr. Ansell returned, looking a little more cheerful.

"Everything is being given by the Bundercombe Reaping Company," he announced, "and Mr. Bundercombe's city agent is on the spot prepared to book orders for the machine. It seems that Mr. Bundercombe has backed himself at ten to one in ten-pound notes to beat Mr. Jonas by half an hour, each taking half the field."

"Who's ahead?" Eve asked excitedly.

"Mr. Bundercombe is well ahead," Mr. Ansell replied, "and they say that he can do better still if he tries. It looks rather," Mr. Ansell concluded, dropping his voice, "as though he were trying to make the thing last out. Afterward they are all going to sit down to a free meal - that is, if any of them are able to sit down," he added, with a glance round the field. "Hello! Here's Harrison."

Mr. Harrison, recognizing us, descended from his car and came across. He shook hands with Eve, at whom he glanced in a somewhat peculiar fashion.

"Mr. Walmsley," he said, "a week ago we were rather proud of having inveigled away one of your adherents. All I can say at the present moment is that we should have been better satisfied if you had left Mr. Bundercombe in town."

"Why, he's been speaking against me at nearly every one of your meetings!" I protested.

"That's all very well," Mr. Harrison complained; "but he's not what I should call a convincing speaker. He is a democrat all right, and a people's man - and all the rest of it; but he hasn't got quite the right way of advocating our principles. I have been obliged to ask him to discontinue public speaking until after the election. The fact of it is, I really believe he's cost us a good many more votes than he's gained. All he says is very well; but when he sits down one feels that our people are all for what they can get out of it - and yours are prepared to give their services for nothing."

"What's all this mean?" I asked, waving my hand toward the field.

Mr. Harrison looked at me very steadily indeed. Then he looked at Eve. I can only hope that my own expression was as guileless as Eve's.

"I told you about that hint we were obliged to give Mr. Bundercombe," Mr. Harrison went on. "I suppose this is the result of it. He seems to have bewitched the whole of Little Bildborough. There's Jonas there, who was due to speak in four places today - he will take no notice of anybody. I walked by the side of his machine, begging him to get down and come and keep his engagements, and he took no more notice of me than if I'd been a rabbit!

"There's his cousin, who has more hold upon the nonconformists of the district than any man I know - sitting under a hedge drinking out of a tumbler! There are at least a score of men with their eyes glued on that tent who ought to be hard at work in the district. I am beginning to doubt whether they'll even be in in time to vote!"

"Well, we must be getting on, anyway," I said. "See you later, Mr. Harrison!"

Mr. Harrison nodded a little gloomily and we glided off. Eve squeezed my hand under the rug.

"Isn't dad a dear!" she murmured in my ear.

Eve was one of the first to congratulate me when, late that night, the results came in and I found that by a majority of twenty-seven votes I had been elected the member for the division.

"Aren't you glad now, Paul, dear, that we brought father down to keep him out of mischief?" she whispered.

Mr. Bundercombe himself held out his hand.

"Paul," he said, "I congratulate you, my boy! I was on the other side; but I can take a licking with the best of them. Congratulate you heartily!"

He held out his hand and gripped mine. Once more he winked.

CHAPTER XII

THE EMANCIPATION OF LOUIS

At about half past ten the following morning I turned into Prince's Gardens, to find a four-wheel cab drawn up outside the door of Mr. Bundercombe's house. On the roof was a dressing case made of some sort of compressed cane and covered with linen. Accompanying it was a black tin box, on which was painted, in white letters: "Hannah Bundercombe, President W.S.F." Standing by the door was a footman with an article in his hand that I believe is called a grip, which, in the present instance, I imagine took the place of a dressing case.

I surveyed these preparations with some interest. The temporary departure of Mrs. Bundercombe would, I felt, have an enlivening influence upon the establishment. As I turned in at the gate Mrs. Bundercombe herself appeared. She was followed by a young woman who looked distinctly bored and whom I was not at first able to place. Mrs. Bundercombe was in a state of unusual excitement.

"Say, Mr. Walmsley," she began, and her voice seemed to come from her forehead - it was so shrill and nasal; "how long will it take me to get to St. Pancras?"

I looked at the four-wheeler, on the roof of which another servant was now arranging a typewriter in its tin case.

"I should say about thirty-five minutes - in that!" I replied. "A taxi would do it in a quarter of an hour."

"None of your taxis for me!" Mrs. Bundercombe declared warmly. "I am not disposed to trust myself to a piece of machinery that can be made to tell any sort of lies. I like to pay my fare and no more. If thirty-five minutes will get me to St. Pancras, then I guess I'll make my train."

"You are leaving us for a few days?" I remarked, suddenly catching a glimpse of a face like a round moon beaming at me from the window.

"I have received a dispatch," Mrs. Bundercombe announced, drawing a letter with pride from an article that I believe she called her reticule, "signed by the secretary of the Women's League of Freedom, asking me to address their members at a meeting to be held at Leeds to-night."

"Very gratifying!" I murmured.

"How the woman knew that I was in England," Mrs. Bundercombe continued, carefully replacing the missive, "I cannot imagine; but I suppose these things get about. In any case I felt it my duty to go. Some of us, Mr. Walmsley," she added, regarding me with a severe air, "think of little else save the various pleasures we are able to cram into our lives day by day. Others are always ready to listen to the call of duty."

"I wish you a pleasant journey, Mrs. Bundercombe," I said, raising my hat. "I suppose I shall find Eve in?"

"No doubt you will!" she snapped.

I glanced at the depressed young woman.

"I am taking a temporary secretary with me," Mrs. Bundercombe explained. "Recent reports of my speeches in this country have been so unsatisfactory that I have lost confidence in the Press. I am taking an experienced shorthand-writer with me, who will furnish the various journals with a verbatim report of what I say."

"Much more satisfactory, I am sure," I agreed, edging toward the house. "I wish you a successful meeting, Mrs. Bundercombe. You mustn't miss your train!"

"And I trust," Mrs. Bundercombe concluded, as she turned to enter the cab, "that if you accompany Eve in her shopping expeditions to-day, or during my absence, you will not encourage her in any fresh extravagances."

I made my way into the house and entered the morning room as the cab drove off. Mr. Bundercombe and Eve were waltzing. Mr. Bundercombe paused at my entrance and wiped his forehead. He was very hot.

"A little ebullition of feeling, my dear Paul," he explained, "on seeing you. You met Mrs. Bundercombe? You have heard the news?"

"I gathered," I remarked, "that Mrs. Bundercombe's sense of duty is taking her to Leeds."

Mr. Bundercombe breathed a resigned sigh.

"We shall be alone," he announced, with ill-concealed jubilation, "if we have any luck at all, for three days! One never knows, though! I propose that we celebrate to-night, unless," he added, with a sudden gloom, "you two want to go off and dine somewhere alone."

"Not likely!" I assured him quickly.

"Daddy!" Eve exclaimed reproachfully.

Mr. Bundercombe cheered up.

"Then, if you're both agreeable," he proposed, "let us go and pay Luigi a visit. I have rather a fancy to show him a reestablished Mr. Bundercombe. You know, I sometimes think," he went on, "that Luigi was beginning to regard me with suspicion!"

"There isn't any doubt about it," I observed dryly.

"We will dine there to-night," Mr. Bundercombe decided, "that is, if you two are willing."

I hesitated for a moment. Eve was looking at me for my decision.

"I really see no reason why we shouldn't go there," I said. "I have to take Eve to some rather dull relatives for luncheon, and I suppose we shall be shopping afterward. It will brighten up the day."

"We will give Luigi no intimation of our coming," Mr. Bundercombe suggested with relish. "We shall be in no hurry; so we can order our dinner when we arrive there. At eight o'clock?"

"At eight o'clock!" I agreed.

"More presents, Paul!" Eve informed me, taking my arm. "Come along and help me unpack! Isn't it fun?"

Luigi's reception of us that night was most gratifying. He escorted us to the best table in the place, from which he ruthlessly seized the mystic label that kept it from the onslaughts of less privileged guests. He congratulated me upon my parliamentary honors and my engagement in the same breath.

It was perfectly clear to me that Luigi knew all about us. He addressed Mr. Bundercombe with an air of deep respect in which was visible, too, an air of relieved apprehension. He took our order himself, with the aid of an assistant *maître d'hôtel*, at whom Mr. Bundercombe glanced with some surprise.

"Where is Louis?" he inquired.

"Gone - left!" Luigi answered.

Mr. Bundercombe was obviously disappointed.

"Say, is that so!" he exclaimed, "Why, I thought he was a fixture! Been here a long time, had'nt he?"

"Nearly twelve years," Luigi admitted.

"Has he got a restaurant of his own?" Mr. Bundercombe asked.

Luigi shook his head.

"On the contrary, sir," he replied, "I think Louis has gone off his head. He has taken a very much inferior post at a very inferior place. A restaurant of a different class altogether - not at all *comme il faut*; a little place for the multitude - Giatron's, in Soho. The foolishness of it - for all his old clients must be useless! No one would eat in such a hole. It is most mysterious!"

We dined well and gayly. Mr. Bundercombe renewed many restaurant acquaintances and I am quite sure he thoroughly enjoyed himself. Every now and then, however, a shadow rested on his face. Watching him, I felt quite certain of the reason. It was only during the last few weeks that I had begun to realize the immense good nature of the man. He was worrying about Louis.

We sat there until nearly ten o'clock. When we rose to go Mr. Bundercombe turned to us. "Say," he asked, a little diffidently, "would you people object to just dropping in at this Giatron's? Or will you go off somewhere by yourselves and meet me afterward?"

"We will go wherever you go, dad," Eve declared. "We are not going to leave you alone when we do have an evening off."

"I should like to find out about Louis myself," I interposed. "I always thought he was the best *maître d'hôtel* in London."

We drove to Giatron's and found it in a back street - a shabby, unpretentious-looking place, with a front that had once been white, but that was now grimy in the extreme. The windows were hung with little curtains in the French fashion, whose freshness had also long departed. The restaurant itself was low and teeming with the odor of past dinners. At this hour it was almost empty. Several untidy-looking waiters were rearranging tables. In the middle of the room Louis was standing.

He recognized us with a little start, though he made no movement whatever in our direction. He was certainly a changed being. He stood and looked at us as though we were ghosts. Mr. Bundercombe waved his hand in friendly fashion. It was not until then that Louis, with marked unwillingness, came forward to greet us.

"Come to see your new quarters, Louis!" Mr. Bundercombe said cheerfully. "Find us a table and serve us some of your special coffee. We will dine here another evening."

Louis showed us to a table and handed us over to the care of an unwholesome-looking German waiter, with only a very brief interchange of courtesies. And then, with a word of excuse, he darted away. Mr. Bundercombe looked after him wonderingly.

The coffee was brought by the waiter and served without Louis' reappearance. The effect of his absence on Mr. Bundercombe, however, was only to make him more determined than ever to get at the bottom of whatever mystery there might be.

"Just tell Louis, the *maître d'hôtel*, I wish to speak to him," he instructed the waiter.

The man departed. Ten minutes passed, but there was no sign of Louis. Mr. Bundercombe sent another and more imperative message. This time Louis obeyed it. As he crossed the room a little hesitatingly toward us, it was almost sad to notice the alteration in his appearance. At Luigi's he had been so smart, so upright, so well dressed. Here he was a changed being. His hair needed cutting; his linen was no longer irreproachable; his clothes were dusty and out of shape. The man seemed to have lost all care of himself and all pride in his work. When at last he reached the table Mr. Bundercombe did not beat about the bush.

"Louis," he said, "we have been to Stephano's tonight for the first time for some weeks. I came along here to see you because of what Luigi told me. Now you can just take this from me: You've got to tell me the truth. There's something wrong with you! What is it?"

Louis extended his hands. He was making his one effort.

"There is nothing wrong with me," he declared. "I left Stephano's to - as they say in this country - better myself. I am in charge here - next to Monsieur Giatron himself. If Monsieur Giatron should go back to Italy I should be manager. It seemed like a good post. Perhaps I was foolish to leave."

"Louis," Mr. Bundercombe protested, "I guess I didn't come round here to listen to lies. You and I had some little dealings together and I feel I've the right to insist on the truth. Now, then, don't give us any more trouble - there's a good fellow! If you'd rather talk to me alone invite me into the office or behind that desk."

Louis looked round the room, which was almost empty, save for the waiters preparing the tables for supper.

"Mr. Bundercombe," he said, with a little gesture of resignation, "it is because of those dealings that I came to trouble."

Mr. Bundercombe eyed him steadily.

"Go on!" he ordered.

Louis moved closer still to the table.

"It was those banknotes, Mr. Bundercombe," he confessed. "You gave me one packet to be destroyed in the kitchen. I obeyed; but I looked at them first. Never did I see such wonderful work! Those notes - every one seemed real! Every one, as I put it into the fire, gave my heart a pang.

"And then, the other time - when you slipped them under the table to me because Mr. Cullen was about! I took them, too, to the fire. I destroyed one, two, three, four, five - one dozen - two dozen; and then I came to the last two or three, and my fingers - they went slow. I could not bear it. I thought what could be done. My wife she was not well. I could send her to Italy. I owe a little bill. The tips - they had not been good lately. Behold! There was one ten-pound note left when all the others were destroyed. I put him in my waistcoat pocket."

"Go on!" Mr. Bundercombe said encouragingly. "No one is blaming you. Upon my word, it sounds natural enough."

Louis' voice grew a little bolder.

"For some time I hesitated how to change it. Then one

day I came here to see my friend Giatron - we came together from Italy. I hand him the note. I ask him please change. He give me the change and I stay to have a drink with the head waiter, who is a friend of mine. Presently Giatron comes out. He calls me into the office. Then I begin to tremble. He looks at me and I tremble more.

"Then he knows that he have got me. Giatron's a very cruel man, Mr. Bundercombe. He make hard terms. He made me give up my good place at Luigi's. He made me come here and be his head man. He gives me half as much as Luigi and there are no tips; besides which the place offends me every moment of the day. The service, the food, the wines - everything is cheap and bad. I take no pride in my work.

"I go to Giatron and I pray him to let me go. But not so! I know my work well. He thinks that I will bring clients. Nowhere else could he get a head man so good as I at the wages of a common waiter. So I stay here - a slave!"

The man's story was finished. In a sense it seemed ordinary enough, and yet both Eve and I felt a curious thrill of sympathy as he finished. There was something almost dramatic in the man's sad voice, his depressed bearing, the story of this tragedy that had come so suddenly into his life. One looked round and realized the truth of all he had said. One realized something, even, of the bitterness of his daily life.

Mr. Bundercombe sipped his coffee thoughtfully.

"Tell me why you did not come to me or write, Louis?" he asked.

The man stretched out his hands.

"But it was to you, sir, that I had broken my word!" he pointed out. "When you gave me that first little bundle you looked at me so steadfastly - when you told me that every scrap was to be destroyed; and I promised - I promised you faithfully. And you asked me afterward about that last batch. You said to me: 'Louis, you are sure that they are all quite gone? Remember that there is trouble in the possession of them!' And I told you a lie!"

Mr. Bundercombe coughed and poured himself out a little more of the coffee.

"Louis," he declared, "you are a fool! You are a blithering idiot! You are a jackass! It never occurred to me before. I am the guilty one for placing such a temptation in your way. Now where's this Monsieur Giatron of yours?"

Louis looked at him wonderingly. There was a dawn of hope in his face, blended with a startled fear.

"He arrives in ten minutes," he announced. "He comes down for the supper. He is here."

Mr. Bundercombe glanced round. A stout man, with a black mustache, had entered the room. His eyes fell at once on the little group. Mr. Bundercombe turned round.

"So that is Monsieur Giatron?"

Louis bowed. Mr. Bundercombe beckoned the proprietor to approach.

"An old patron of Luigi's," Mr. Bundercombe explained, introducing himself - "come round to see our friend Louis, here."

"Delighted, I am very sure!" Mr. Giatron exclaimed, bowing to all of us. "It will be a great pleasure to us to do the very best possible for any of Louis' friends."

Mr. Bundercombe rose to his feet. He pointed to the little glass-framed office at the other side of the room.

"Mr. Giatron," he said, "I have always been a great patron of Louis. You and I must have a chat. Will you not invite us into your little office and show us whether there is not something better to be found than this coffee? We will take a glass of brandy together and drink success to your restaurant."

Giatron hastened to lead the way. Eve, in response to a glance from her father, remained at the table; but I followed Mr. Bundercombe. We went into the office; Giatron himself placed three glasses upon the desk and produced from a cupboard a bottle of what appeared to be very superior brandy. Mr. Bundercombe sipped his with relish. Then he glanced at the closed door.

"Mr. Giatron," he began, "I have been having a chat with Louis. He has told me of his troubles - told me the reason for his leaving Luigi and accepting this post with you."

Giatron paused, with the bottle suspended in mid-air. He slowly set it down. A frown appeared on his face.

"Mind you," Mr. Bundercombe continued, "I am not sympathizing with Louis. If what he said is true I am inclined to think you have been very merciful."

Giatron recovered his confidence.

"He tried - Louis tried - my old friend," he complained, "to take advantage of me; to enrich himself at my expense by means of a false note."

"That is the only point," Mr. Bundercombe said.

"Was the note bad? Do you know I can scarcely bring myself to believe it!"

The restaurant keeper smiled. Very deliberately he produced a great bunch of keys from his pocket and opened the safe, which stood in a corner of the office. Mr. Bundercombe whispered a scarcely audible word in my ear and became absorbed once more in the brandy. Presently Giatron returned. He laid on the desk and smoothed out carefully what was to all appearances a ten-pound note.

"If you will examine that carefully, sir," he begged, "you will see that it is the truth. That note, he is very well made; but he is not a good Bank of England note."

Mr. Bundercombe slowly adjusted his glasses, placed the note in front of him and smoothed it carefully with his large hand. "This is very interesting," he murmured. "Allow me to make a close examination. I've seen some high-class printing in my - "

Giatron started as though he were shot and jumped round toward me. With unpardonable clumsiness I had upset my glass in leaning over to look at the note.

"I'm awfully sorry!" I exclaimed, glancing ruefully at my trousers. "Would you give me a napkin quickly?"

Giatron hastened to the door of the office and called to a passing waiter. The napkin was soon procured and I rubbed myself dry. The restaurant keeper returned to the desk at Mr. Bundercombe's side.

"All I can say," Mr. Bundercombe declared, as he drew away from the note, which he had been examining, "is that I do not wonder you were deceived, Mr. Giatron. This note is the most perfect imitation I have ever seen in my life. A wicked piece of work, sir!"

"You recognize the fact, however, that the note is beyond question counterfeit?" Mr. Giatron persisted.

"I fear you are right," Mr. Bundercombe admitted. "There is a slight imperfection. Yes, yes - a very bad business, Mr. Giatron! We must come here often and try to see whether we cannot make you a second Luigi."

Giatron returned to the safe with the note, which he carefully locked up.

"Very excellent brandy!" Mr. Bundercombe pronounced warmly. "You will see a great deal more of us, my friend. I promise you that. We shall haunt you!"

Mr. Giatron bowed to the ground.

"You are always very welcome - and the young lady!"

We rejoined Eve, paid our bill, and made our way to the door. Louis, looking very pathetic, was in the background. Mr. Bundercombe beckoned to him.

"Louis, you can give your shark of an employer a week's notice to-night! I have the note in my pocket," he whispered. "It's cost me a good one; but I owed you that. On Monday week, Louis, I shall order my dinner from you at Luigi's."

The man's face was wonderful! He came a little closer. He was shaking at the knees, his hands were trembling, and his mouth was twitching. "Mr. Bundercombe," he pleaded hoarsely, "you would not deceive me!"

Mr. Bundercombe looked at him steadfastly.

"On my honor, Louis, the note is in my pocket, already torn in four pieces when I put my hand into my waistcoat pocket to pay my bill. In three minutes it will be in a hundred pieces - gone! You need have no fear. The note Mr. Giatron is guarding so carefully is a very excellent ten-pound note of my own."

At a quarter to eight on the following Monday week Mr. Bundercombe and I entered Luigi's restaurant. Louis himself advanced to greet us - the old Louis, whose linen was irreproachable, whose bearing and deportment and gracious smile all denoted the Louis of old. Mr. Bundercombe ordered dinner and beckoned Louis to come a little nearer.

"Was there any trouble?" he inquired.

"For me, no," Louis replied; "but Monsieur Giatron - never, never have I seen a man like it! He fetched out the note. 'Now,' he said, 'I take your notice! You take mine! Ring up the police! Or shall I?'

"Then I tell him. I say: 'I don't believe the note bad at all!' He laughed at me. He got it from the safe and laid it on the desk. 'Not bad!' he jeered. 'Not bad!' Then he stood looking at it.

"Mr. Bundercombe, I see his face change. His mouth came wide open; his eyes looked as though they would drop out. He bend over that note. He looked at it and looked at it; and then he looked at me.

"'I don't believe that note ever was bad!' I say. 'I told you when you charged me I didn't believe it. That is why I have made up my mind to give you notice, to go away from here. And if that note is bad then you can put me in prison.'

"Monsieur Giatron - he went back to the safe. He rummaged round among a pile of papers and soon he came out again. He was looking pasty-colored. 'Louis,' he said, 'some one has been very clever! You can go to hell!' And so, Mr. Bundercombe," Louis wound up, beaming, "here I am!"

CHAPTER XIII

"THE SHORN LAMB"

I never remembered seeing Mr. Bundercombe look more cheerful than when, at his urgent summons, I left Eve in the drawing-room and made my way into the study. He was standing on the hearthrug, with the tails of his morning coat drooping over his arms and an expression on his face that I can only describe as cherubic. Seated on chairs, a yard or so away from him, were two visitors of whom at first glance I formed a most unfavorable opinion. One was a flashily dressed, middle-aged man, with fair mustache, puffy cheeks, and a superfluity of jewelry. The other I might at first have taken for an undertaker's mute. He had an exceedingly red nose, watery eyes, and was dressed in deep mourning.

"Paul," Mr. Bundercombe said, "let me introduce you to Captain Duncan Bannister and Mr. Cheape, his solicitor."

The two men rose and bowed in turn. I found it difficult to maintain a tolerant attitude, but I did my best.

"These two gentlemen," Mr. Bundercombe continued cheerfully, "have come round to blackmail me."

E. Phillips Oppenheim

"Sir!" Captain Bannister exclaimed, with a great show of anger.

"Mr. Bundercombe!" the person called Mr. Cheape echoed.

They made rather a poor show of it, however. Mr. Bundercombe, wholly unperturbed by their righteous indignation, smiled still benignly upon them.

"Come, come!" he expostulated. "This is a business interview. Why mince words?"

Captain Bannister rose to his feet. He turned toward me.

"Mr. Bundercombe," he explained, "either willfully or otherwise, misinterprets the object of our coming. It is possible that his nationality may have something to do with it. I have always understood that the standard among Americans with regard to affairs of honor is scarcely so high as in this country."

"Mr. Bundercombe has a habit of taking a common-sense view of things," I remarked. "I cannot criticize his attitude, because I am ignorant of the particulars. Since he has sent for me, however, I presume that I am to be informed."

"Quite so - quite so!" Mr. Bundercombe murmured. "You go ahead, Captain Bannister. You tell your story."

"My story," Captain Bannister said, "is told in a very few words. I made the acquaintance of Mr. Bundercombe in the smoking room at the Milan some months ago. We met several times; and on one occasion I presented him to a friend of mine, the widow of a colonel in the Indian Army, Mrs. Delaporte."

At this stage, Mr. Bundercombe, who was quite irrepressible, winked at me slowly. I took no notice of him whatever.

"On the particular evening to which I refer," Captain Bannister continued, "it was suggested, by Mrs. Delaporte, I think, that we should go round to her rooms and play *chemin de fer*. There were five of us altogether - Mr. Bundercombe, Mrs. Delaporte, myself, a Mr. Dimsdale, and the Honorable Montague Pelham, a young gentleman of the best family. When we arrived at Mrs. Delaporte's rooms, however, it transpired that Mr. Bundercombe was wholly ignorant of *chemin de fer*, and the game was accordingly changed to poker.

"In the course of the game I was shocked to detect Mr. Bundercombe cheating. For Mrs. Delaporte's sake I conceived it best to try and hush up the matter entirely. I looked upon Mr. Bundercombe as a card sharper of the ordinary type, and I simply blamed myself for having introduced him to my friends. I accordingly made some excuse to terminate the party."

"Did any one else besides yourself," I inquired, "observe this alleged irregularity?"

"Both Mrs. Delaporte and Mr. Dimsdale distinctly saw the very flagrant piece of cheating that first attracted my attention," Captain Bannister declared. "They understood at once the position when I suggested the termination of the game. Our party broke up hurriedly.

Since that day I have not seen Mr. Bundercombe."

I turned toward my prospective father-in-law. Mr. Bundercombe for the first time was looking a little annoyed.

"Do you mean to tell me," he said, addressing Captain Bannister, "that both that young jay Dimsdale and Mrs. Delaporte saw me pass up that ace?"

"Without a doubt," Captain Bannister assented, a little taken aback.

"Guess my fingers must be getting a bit clumsy," Mr. Bundercombe sighed. "Well, well! There the matter is."

"But, Mr. Bundercombe," I asked seriously, "what have you to say in reply to Captain Bannister's statement?"

"Don't seem to me there's much to be said," Mr. Bundercombe replied.

"But he accuses you of cheating!" I exclaimed.

"Oh, I cheated all right!" Mr. Bundercombe admitted readily.

Captain Bannister turned toward me triumphantly.

"After that confession from Mr. Bundercombe before witnesses," he said, "I do not imagine that our case will require very much more proof."

I was completely nonplussed - Mr. Bundercombe's

confession was so ready, his demeanor so unalterably good-tempered. I went on to ask, however, what certainly seemed to me the most important question under the circumstances.

"If you were content, Captain Bannister," I inquired, "to let the matter drop a few months ago, why are you here now?"

"Aha!" Mr. Bundercombe exclaimed. "Put his finger on the crux of the whole affair straight off! Smart young fellow, my son-in-law that is to be! Now, then, Captain Bannister and Mr. Cheape, speak up like men and let us know the truth. You let me walk out of that flat, Captain Bannister, and were jolly glad to see the back of me. Why this visit with a legal adviser, and both of you with faces as long as fiddles?"

Captain Bannister ignored Mr. Bundercombe and addressed me.

"Mr. Bundercombe," he said, "calling himself, by the by, Mr. Parker, as an American card sharper was of no interest to us. We were simply ashamed and disgusted to think that we should have permitted such a person the entrée to our society. When we discovered, however, that, instead of being a professional card sharper," Captain Bannister continued, with emphasis, "Mr. Bundercombe enjoys a recognized position in society, and that he is reputed to be a man of great wealth, the affair assumes an altogether different complexion."

"Worth going for, ain't I?" Mr. Bundercombe chuckled.

"I feel sure, Mr. Walmsley," Captain Bannister continued, "that some portion of your sympathy, at any rate, as an English gentleman of social distinction, will be with us in this matter. The affair we were content to let drop against Mr. Parker, the adventurer, we feel it our duty to pursue against Mr. Bundercombe, the millionaire."

"We would save time," I remarked coldly, "if you were to put your demands into plain words. What is it you want or expect from Mr. Bundercombe?"

"Not what you appear to think, sir," Captain Bannister replied stiffly. "We require from Mr. Bundercombe a written confession and his resignation from the Sidney Club."

"The what club?" I asked dubiously.

"The Sidney Club," Captain Bannister repeated, with dignity. "The club in question may not be very large, but it is quite well known, and I had the misfortune to act as Mr. Bundercombe's sponsor there."

I glanced toward my prospective father-in-law. He nodded.

"They put me up for some sort of a pothouse," he admitted, "and I handed over a tenner, I think it was, for my subscription. Rotten little hole somewhere near the Haymarket! I've never been in since. I'll resign, with pleasure!"

"And write a confession of your misdemeanor, sir?" Captain Bannister persisted.

Mr. Bundercombe scratched his chin.

"I'll write an account of the whole affair," he remarked dryly.

Captain Bannister took up his hat.

"I regret," he declared, "that Mr. Bundercombe's attitude does not encourage a continuation of this conversation. We will not detain you further, gentlemen."

Mr. Cheape also rose. They moved toward the door.

"Much obliged to you for calling," Mr. Bundercombe said hospitably. "Drop in and have a little game of cards with me any afternoon you like. I am a bit out of practice, but I fancy I am still in your class."

Captain Bannister turned round suddenly. He replaced his hat upon the table and stood with folded arms.

"Sir," he announced, "I have changed my mind. You have insulted me. Five minutes ago I was prepared to treat you like a gentleman. I would have accepted your resignation from the Sidney Club and your written apology. Now I have changed my mind. You have slandered me, both by imputation and directly."

"How much?" Mr. Bundercombe asked cheerfully.

"Five thousand pounds!" Captain Bannister answered firmly.

"How much more if I call you a lying, card-sharping swindler ? " Mr. Bundercombe demanded , with unabated good humor.

Captain Bannister looked dangerous, but he ignored the question.

"You have your terms, sir," he said. "Unless you are prepared to hand over the sum of five thousand pounds, my solicitor, Mr. Cheape here, will at once commence proceedings against you with reference to the affair in Mrs. Delaporte's flat. Remember, we have four witnesses to bring into court as to your having cheated - not including your son-in-law here, who heard your confession. For any countercharge you might be disposed to make," Captain Bannister concluded, "you have not a single scrap of evidence."

"Got me on toast, haven't they, Paul?" Mr. Bundercombe observed cheerfully. "Five thousand pounds is a lot of money, Captain Bannister," he added. "I'll pay your taxi fare back to wherever you came from. That's my best offer."

Captain Bannister turned toward the door.

"Come along, Mr. Cheape!" he said. "You know my address, sir. Talk this matter over with your - with Mr. Walmsley, if you please. If we hear nothing from you on Monday morning a writ will be issued."

"Before Monday," Mr. Bundercombe declared, in a hollow voice, "my body will be found in the Thames. Kick 'em out, Walmsley, and look after the coats in the hall!"

I infused a shade more civility into my leavetaking than Mr. Bundercombe's words invited. As soon as the door was closed behind the two men I returned to the study. Mr. Bundercombe was still standing upon the hearthrug, but the smile had faded from his lips. He looked at me a little anxiously.

"Rotten lot of thieves!" he remarked. "I told you they were here for blackmail."

"It's a beastly affair," I pointed out gloomily, "You see, they've nothing to lose, with a lawyer who's standing in with them, in taking the case into court; and you're just up for a couple of very good clubs. What did happen?"

"Simple as ABC!" Mr. Bundercombe explained. "You see these two fellows, Dimsdale and Pelham, really looked like mugs. I knew that Bannister was a wrong 'un from the first; and Mrs. Delaporte, of course, was in the thing. When they proposed a game of cards I chipped in, thinking to watch the fun. When we started playing Dimsdale and Pelham were the losers. Then they began to get at me. Bannister palmed a king into his hand and I palmed an ace. That seemed fair enough, eh?"

Mr. Bundercombe's expression as he looked at me was the expression of an appealing child. I bit my lip.

"A minute or two later I tumbled to the whole situation," he went on. "Dimsdale and Pelham weren't jays at all. It was a gang of four and they raked me in for the mug. After I'd tumbled to that I must confess I took some interest in the game. If they had given me another quarter of an hour I should have won every chip there was going. My boy," Mr. Bundercombe went on, a sudden grin transfiguring his expressive countenance, "it was worth a fortune to see their faces!

"I was a bit out of practice, but I guarantee I'd make a living with my fingers and a pack of cards anywhere yet and defy detection. I had 'em all guessing before long; and, Paul, you should have seen their faces when they tumbled to it! I tell you they bundled me out in double-quick time and I laughed all the way home. Four sharks to pitch upon me as a victim!"

He began to laugh again, but the sight of my grave face checked him. He at once assumed the appearance of a penitent.

"Where did you come across them again?" I asked.

"I met Mrs. Delaporte the other day," he said, "down at Ranelagh. We chatted a little while. I couldn't feel any ill-will against the woman - I'd enjoyed my evening so thoroughly. Then some people stopped and talked to me, and she found out who I was. Soon afterward she began to throw out hints of a willingness to marry again. Perhaps I wasn't very tactful. Anyway she seemed a little huffed when she left me - and here we are! Say, do you think those joshers can do anything?"

"It rather depends," I replied, "upon their own reputations. You'd better let me make a few inquiries. I'll have to get off now, Eve's waiting. I'll call round and see my solicitor later in the day."

"Shame to bother you," Mr. Bundercombe regretted. "So long!"

The affair Mr. Bundercombe had treated with his customary light-heartedness seemed likely to develop most unpleasantly. Within forty-eight hours he was the recipient of a writ from the firm of solicitors with which Mr. Cheape was connected; and, though inquiries went to prove that Captain Bannister, Mrs. Delaporte and their associates were certainly not people of the highest respectability, there was yet nothing definite against them. My solicitor, to whom I took Mr. Bundercombe, most regretfully advised him to settle out of court.

"The friends Mr. Bundercombe is now making and may make in later life," the lawyer remarked, "will certainly not appreciate the adventurous spirit that - er - induced him to make acquaintances among a certain class of people. Therefore, in the interests of my client, Mr. Walmsley, as well as your own, Mr. Bundercombe," he concluded, "I am afraid I must advise you, very much against my own inclinations, to settle this matter."

Mr. Bundercombe left the lawyer's office thoroughly depressed.

"It isn't the money!" he declared gloomily. "It's being bested by this little gang of thieves that irritates me!"

"I am sure," I told him, "that Mr. Wymans' advice is sound. If the case goes into court and comes up before the committee - even of a rotten club like the Sidney - I am afraid you would have to withdraw your membership from the other places; and you might find the affair continually cropping up and causing you annoyance."

Mr. Bundercombe heaved a mighty sigh.

"Well, we've got two days left," he said. "If nothing happens before then I'll pay up."

E. Phillips Oppenheim

* * * * *

Mr. Bundercombe rang me up on the morning of the last day appointed for his decision.

"We've got a conference on, Paul," he announced dejectedly. "Will you come round here for me at a quarter to eleven?"

I assented, and arrived at the house in Prince's Gardens a few minutes before that time. Eve met me in the hall.

"Please tell me, dear," she begged, as she drew me into the morning room, "why daddy is so low-spirited!"

"It isn't anything serious," I assured her. "It's just a little trouble arising from one of his adventures. We shall get out of it all right."

"Poor daddy!" she exclaimed. "I am sure he has had no sleep for two nights. I heard him walking up and down his room."

"Well, it will all be over to-day," I promised. "After all, it only means a little money."

"Daddy does so hate to get the worst of anything," she sighed; "and I am afraid, from the looks of his face, that this time he's in a fix."

"I am afraid so, too," I agreed. "Never mind; we have done the best we can, and we are going to settle it up once and for all to-day. Perhaps he'll tell you about it afterward."

We heard a door slam and Mr. Bundercombe's voice.

"He is asking for you," Eve whispered. "Hurry along and come back as soon as you've got this business over."

I found Mr. Bundercombe exceedingly chastened, but in all other respects his usual self.

"We are calling for Mr. Wymans," he said, "in Lincoln's Inn Fields, and afterward we are going round to Mrs. Delaporte's flat. We are going to meet Bannister there and his lawyer."

"Why do we concern ourselves in the matter at all?" I asked as we drove off. "I don't see why we can't leave the lawyers to do this final settlement."

Mr. Bundercombe shook his head.

"You leave too much to lawyers in this country," he remarked. "We generally like to see the thing through ourselves over at home, even if we take a lawyer along. This is an unpleasant business, if you like; but there's no good in shirking it."

We called for Mr. Wymans and drove on to Mrs. Delaporte's flat. We were at once admitted into an overheated and overperfumed room and found Captain Bannister, Mrs. Delaporte, and Mr. Cheape awaiting us. Their demeanor betokened anxiety. Mrs. Delaporte alone made a little conversation; and, the habits of a lifetime asserting themselves, she made eyes at Mr. Bundercombe.

Mr. Bundercombe, however, conducted himself very much like the deacon of a chapel in the presence of his minister. His natural good humor seemed to have departed. His manners matched the unusual solemnity of his attire.

"Madam," he said, bowing to Mrs. Delaporte, "Mr. Cheape and Captain Bannister, I have suggested this conference because I believe in settling these affairs myself and not leaving everything to lawyers - no disrespect to present company. I have made an idiot of myself and I am ready to pay - a certain amount."

Mr. Cheape rose to his feet. He was sitting in front of a writing desk, with a clean sheet of paper in front of him, as though prepared to take notes of the proceedings.

"So that there may be no possible misunderstanding," he intervened, "my clients will take not a penny less than the five thousand pounds mentioned."

"And I," Mr. Bundercombe declared sadly but very firmly, "will not give a penny more than four thousand pounds."

Mr. Cheape shrugged his shoulders as though to intimate that the conference was at an end. Captain Bannister made a few remarks to the effect that if he had not been a moderate man, and willing to conduct the affair in a gentlemanly manner, he should have asked for ten thousand. Mrs. Delaporte alluded to five thousand pounds as though the amount represented the outcome of a day's shopping. It was astonishing how little they seemed to regard the value of money!

"Now," Mr. Bundercombe went on, "if I've brought you all together here on false pretenses, I am sorry. There's nothing to be done in that case but to say good morning and meet in the law court. But," he added, striking the back of a chair with his clenched fist and looking more like Napoleon than I had ever seen him, "I swear, by the word of Joseph H. Bundercombe, which has never yet been broken, that I will not hand over one cent more than four thousand pounds!"

The protests were this time a little weaker. Mr. Bundercombe sat with folded arms, with his eyes fixed upon the ceiling and an air of being altogether disinterested in the proceedings, while the three who comprised the other party whispered together.

Presently Mr. Cheape rose to his feet.

"Mr. Wymans," he began, punctiliously addressing the lawyer first, "and Mr. Bundercombe, my clients are only too anxious to end this unhappy matter. They feel that their demands have been most moderate, but at my advice they have consented to accept a reduction of five hundred pounds."

Mr. Bundercombe rose heavily to his feet.

"Mr. Wymans," he said, "and Paul, come along! I do not bargain. I wish you all good morning."

He turned toward the door and we followed him. It was already opened when we were called back. Captain Bannister and Mr. Cheape were whispering eagerly together. Mr. Cheape rose once more to his feet.

"In order to prove," he announced, "how entirely devoid my clients are of mercenary considerations, they agree, Mr. Bundercombe, to accept the sum of four thousand pounds."

Mr. Bundercombe put down his hat again. Then he drew a sheet of paper from his pocket.

"Condition number one, then," he observed, "is now agreed upon. We proceed to condition number two. Mrs. Delaporte, Captain Bannister, and Mr. Cheape," he went on earnestly, "I have been guilty of an indiscretion the proof of which is in your hands. Having decided to make London my home for a time, I desire once and for all to extinguish all possibility of this affair ever cropping up again in any shape or form."

Mr. Cheape rose to his feet.

"Sir," he said to Mr. Bundercombe, "my clients will give you their written undertaking that the affair shall be consigned to oblivion."

Mr. Bundercombe waved him down.

"My reasons for feeling so strongly on the matter," he continued, "will be appreciated by you, Captain Bannister, as a man of position and in society" - Captain Bannister bowed - "when I tell you that my future son-in-law, Mr. Walmsley, M.P., has proposed me for membership in two of the most exclusive clubs in London. This affair, therefore, must be killed beyond any manner of doubt. I am handing over to you four thousand pounds, which is a very considerable sum; but in return for it I desire that my future immunity be purchased by your signatures to this document."

Mr. Cheape rose at once to his feet. "A document!" he observed. "Let me read it." Mr. Bundercombe handed it over. Mr. Cheape read it out aloud:

"We, the undersigned, desire to apologize most sincerely to Mr. Joseph H. Bundercombe for any allegations we have made against him with regard to a certain episode that took place on March eighteenth, or thereabout, in the flat of Mrs. Delaporte. We admit that we were mistaken in the supposition which we certainly entertained at the time - that Mr. Bundercombe had been guilty of cheating - and we withdraw such allegations unreservedly, and tender our apologies."

"Ridiculous!" Captain Bannister exclaimed.

"Absurd!" Mrs. Delaporte echoed.

"I may add," Mr. Cheape joined in, "that I could not possibly recommend my clients to sign such a document."

Mr. Bundercombe took up his hat.

"When I started out this morning," he declared, "I felt convinced that this conference would come to nothing. I told Mr. Wymans here that I was prepared to settle, but on my own terms - and my own terms only. I don't want any undertaking not to molest me in the future. That isn't good enough. I want to be able to show a document such as you have there, which completely exculpates me from any charge that might at any time be brought. And without it," he added, once more bringing his fist down upon the back of the chair, "I do not part with one penny of my four thousand pounds!"

Mr. Cheape read out a document he himself had

prepared, but Mr. Bundercombe waved it away.

"Come, Paul!" he said to me with a sigh. "Come, Mr. Wymans! I disclaim all responsibility for the failure of this conference. I have done my best. It cannot matter a snap of the fingers to our friends here in what form the document is couched that they give me in exchange for my four thousand pounds. Since they are so particular about a trifle, I have finished with them!"

He led the way toward the door and there was an appearance of finality about his tone and shoulders exceedingly convincing. We had reached the threshold and were, indeed, indulging in a little skirmish as to who should pass through the door first, when Mr. Cheape's resigned voice checked us.

"My clients," he announced slowly, "will sign your document, Mr. Bundercombe. They protest - they protest vigorously against its wording; but they are anxious to show you in how large-spirited and gentlemanly a manner they wish this affair to be concluded. Once more they yield."

Mr. Bundercombe, without any signs of exultation, returned to his former place, put down his hat upon the chair and drew a checkbook from his breast coat pocket.

"If you will give me a seat and a pen," he said, "I will write you a check for the amount."

Captain Bannister stared at the checkbook. He glanced at Mr. Cheape and Mr. Cheape very vigorously shook his head.

"I am sorry," he objected; "but my clients cannot think of accepting a check in settlement of this matter."

Mr. Bundercombe began to show symptoms of annoyance.

"Bless my soul!" he exclaimed. "Isn't the check of Joseph H. Bundercombe good enough for you?"

Mr. Cheape laid his hand soothingly upon Mr. Bundercombe's shoulder.

"It isn't that we doubt your check, sir," he pointed out; "but in a transaction of this sort it is best that no evidences of a lasting nature should exist. A check is not, as you know, legal tender, and a check my clients certainly could not accept."

Mr. Bundercombe folded up his checkbook and replaced it in his pocket.

"Then what are you going to do about it?" he asked.

"Where is your bank?" Mr. Cheape inquired.

"In Pall Mall," Mr. Bundercombe answered.

"Then I am afraid," Mr. Cheape decided, "there is nothing for it but to ask you to repair there and cash your own check."

Mr. Bundercombe rose to his feet.

"All right!" he agreed. "I suppose we had better finish the affair while we are about it. One of you had better come with me."

Captain Bannister promptly volunteered. He and I and Mr. Bundercombe descended the stairs and entered the car. We pulled up in a few minutes at the door of Mr. Bundercombe's bank.

"Will you come in with me?" Mr. Bundercombe invited, turning to Captain Bannister.

Captain Bannister excused himself.

"I will wait here with Mr. Walmsley," he said, "if you will allow me."

Mr. Bundercombe departed inside the bank and reappeared in the course of a few moments. His breast coat pocket was bulging. On our way back he drew out five packets of banknotes, which he counted carefully. Captain Bannister watched him out of the corner of his eye with a hungry expression. We were only absent from the flat altogether about a quarter of an hour, and the rest of the affair was promptly settled. The notes were counted by Mr. Cheape, the document signed by Captain Bannister and Mrs. Delaporte.

"I am sure," Captain Bannister declared, holding the notes in his left hand, "that no one can be more glad than Mrs. Delaporte and myself that this little affair has been concluded so amicably. If you will allow me, Mr. Bundercombe, to offer you a little refreshment - " Mr. Bundercombe sighed.

"Well," he said, "I suppose it's all in the day's work for you people. I don't mind admitting, though, money wasn't so easily earned in my days that I can watch four thousand pounds go without feeling it. Thank you; that'll do nicely," he added, accepting the brandy-and-soda Captain Bannister handed him.

Mr. Wymans looked on with stern disapproval and I must say I sympathized with him. Mr. Bundercombe, however, not only drained the glass with relish but accepted the outstretched hand of Captain Bannister and afterward shook hands also with Mrs. Delaporte.

"If you are passing at any time - " she whispered in his ear.

I had had enough of it and I dragged Mr. Bundercombe away. We drove back to Prince's Gardens in somewhat ominous silence. Mr. Wymans would have taken his leave, but Mr. Bundercombe begged him to come into the library.

"One moment!" he insisted. "James," he said, addressing the butler, "Mr. Wymans will stay to lunch. One moment!"

Mr. Bundercombe went to the telephone. Mechanically he handed me the additional receiver. He asked for a number and presently received a reply.

"Say, is that Captain Bannister I am speaking to?" he said. "I thought I recognized the voice. This is Mr. Bundercombe. Yes, yes! - No, there's nothing we'd forgotten. I just rang you up, though, to give you a word of advice. You want to be just a *leetle* careful where you try to change those notes!"

"What do you mean, sir?" I heard Captain Bannister demand in startled accents. "What do you mean, Mr. Bundercombe?"

"Well," Mr. Bundercombe continued, "those notes are just about the cleverest things I ever came across; but, after all, they aren't exactly the genuine article. I got four thousand pounds' worth of them from a young fellow I was interested in, and I had them put in a safe at my bank so that no one should get into any trouble. It just occurred to me, since we began our little negotiations, that I saw a good way of making use of them. I had only four thousand pounds' worth; so I had to beat you down a bit. However, that'll be all right, captain, only, as I say, use them a bit carefully.... Jove! Ain't he making the telephone sing!" Mr. Bundercombe added, turning to me. "I guess I'll ring off!" He put down the receiver. Once more the accustomed smile was creeping over his face. Mr. Wymans was looking dazed. The butler had entered the room with the cocktails.

"Say, Paul," Mr. Bundercombe expostulated, "you didn't really think I was parting with four thousand pounds to a sloppy gang like that, did you? I knew a young chap who was very clever at making those notes," he explained to Mr. Wymans. "I liked him and converted him; and I sent him over to the States, where he's got a good situation and is working honestly for his living. This was the remainder of his stock. I had 'em lying in the safe deposit of the bank, meaning some day to destroy 'em. You've got that apology all right?"

Mr. Wymans slowly smiled. He raised his glass to his lips.

"You are a very clever man, Mr. Bundercombe!" he said.

CHAPTER XIV

MR. BUNDERCOMBE'S LOVE AFFAIR

Mr. Bundercombe who, notwithstanding his wife's temporary absence in the country, had not been in the best of spirits for several days, during the course of our tête-à-tête dinner at Luigi's became suddenly and unexpectedly animated. The change in him was so noticeable that I leaned forward in my place to see what could have produced it.

Two people had entered the restaurant and were in conversation now with Luigi about a table. Mr. Bundercombe, who in the affairs of every-day life had no idea of concealing his feelings, was regarding them with every appearance of lively interest.

"Paul," he whispered, "you must notice these two people. Watch them - there's a good fellow!"

They took their places at a table almost opposite ours. The girl, though she was more quietly and tastefully dressed and seemed to me to be better looking, I recognized at once as Mr. Bundercombe's companion at Prince's Restaurant on one memorable occasion.

The man I had never seen before. He appeared to be of about medium height; slim, with a sallow skin; dark,

E. Phillips Oppenheim

sleepy eyes, which suggested the foreigner; a mouth that, straight and firm though it was, turned up a little at the corners, as though in contradiction of his somewhat indolent general appearance. He was exceedingly well-dressed and carried himself with the quiet assurance of a man accustomed to moving in the world.

"Most interesting!" Mr. Bundercombe murmured, having with an effort withdrawn his eyes from the pair. "The girl you doubtless recognize. She was once a typist in the office of Messrs. Harding & Densmore. She was quite lately, as I dare say you remember, able to give me some very useful information; in fact it is through her that Mr. Stanley did not leave this country for South Africa with a hundred pounds in his pocket."

"And the man?" I asked.

Mr. Bundercombe was thoroughly enjoying himself. He drew his chair a little closer to mine and waited until he was quite sure that no one was within earshot.

"The man," he replied, "is one of the world's most famous criminals."

"He doesn't look it," I remarked, glancing across the room with some interest.

Mr. Bundercombe smiled.

"Great criminals are not all of the same type," he reminded me reprovingly. "That is where you people who don't understand the cult of criminology make your foolish mistakes. Our friend opposite is, without a doubt, of gentle though not of aristocratic birth. I know nothing of his bringing up, but his instincts do all that is necessary for him. The first time I saw him was in one of the criminal courts in New York. He was being tried for his life for an attempted robbery in Fifth Avenue and the murder of a policeman. He defended himself and did it brilliantly. In the end he got off. There is scarcely a person, however, who doubts but that he was guilty."

I looked across at the subject of our discussion with renewed interest.

"He shot him, I suppose?" I asked.

"On the contrary," Mr. Bundercombe replied, "he throttled him. The man has the sinews of an ox. The second time I saw him was at a dancing-hall in New York. He was there with a very gay party indeed; but one of them, the wealthiest, mysteriously disappeared. Rodwell - Dagger Rodwell was his nickname - came to England. I saw him once or twice just before I visited you down in Bedfordshire. Cullen warned me off him, however; wouldn't let me have a word to say to him."

"He doesn't sound the best companion in the world for your little typist friend," I remarked.

Mr. Bundercombe glanced across the room and at that moment the girl noticed him. She bowed and waved her hand. Mr. Bundercombe responded gallantly.

"I fancy," he murmured, "that she can take care of herself. Come, I really feel that I am in an interesting atmosphere once more."

Mr. Bundercombe's deportment was certainly more

cheerful. For the last week or two he had been depressed. He had paid visits with Eve and myself, and devoted a reasonable amount of time to his wife. The demands on his complete respectability, however, had been irksome. He was too obviously finding no savor in life.

I really was not altogether sorry at first to notice the improvement in his spirits, though my sentiments changed when, a little later in the evening, the girl opposite left her place and came over to us. She greeted Mr. Bundercombe with the most brilliant of smiles and he held her hand quite as long as was necessary. He presented me and I learned that her name was Miss Blanche Spencer.

"I must not stay long," she said, laughing. "The gentleman I am with is a sort of cousin of mine and we don't get on very well; but I mustn't be rude."

Mr. Bundercombe and she seemed to have a good deal to say to each other and presently I noticed that their heads were drawing closer together. The girl dropped her voice. She was proposing something to which Mr. Bundercombe was listening with keen interest. I heard him sigh.

"If it weren't for certain changes," he explained regretfully, "I guess I wouldn't hesitate a moment. But - "

I heard a whispered reference to myself as his daughter's fiancé and an allusion to the continued presence of his wife in London. She nodded sympathetically.

"Now if there were any other way," Mr. Bundercombe concluded, "in which I could still further show my gratitude to you personally for a certain little matter, why I'm all for hearing about it. I consider the balance is still on my side."

She laughed.

"You're really rather a dear!" she declared. "Do you know I am thinking of starting in business for myself?"

"Where, and what as?" Mr. Bundercombe inquired.

I shook open an evening paper and heard no more. The girl's leavetaking, however, a few minutes later, was both reluctant and impressive. I felt it my duty to allude to the matter as soon as we were alone.

"You know, sir," I said, "this helping young women to set up in business is a proceeding that's very likely to be misunderstood over here. I am not in the least sure that even Eve would quite approve."

Mr. Bundercombe smiled the smile of a man of the world.

"One can't tell one's womenkind everything!" he declared grandiloquently.

I was a little puzzled. I felt convinced that Mr. Bundercombe was concealing something from me.

"Furthermore," I continued, feeling it my duty to speak frankly to my future father-in-law, "a man of your position needs to be very careful when he has financial transactions with a good-looking young woman like

Miss Blanche. The young lady herself might take advantage of it."

Mr. Bundercombe appeared to be giving my words full consideration.

"Well, well!" he said, a little vaguely. "We shall see. I don't mind telling you, though, Paul, that I would have nothing to say to her first suggestion - on your account, my boy. There's a scheme on foot in which her interesting companion is concerned, which needs financing. I haven't the least doubt that it is something entirely interesting - probably a mammoth jewel robbery or something of the sort."

I looked across at the man, who seemed to be reproaching the girl for her long absence. Almost at that moment he looked up and our eyes met for a brief instant. There seemed to be nothing in his gaze beyond a measure of polite and not too pointed interest. Nevertheless, when I looked away I begged Mr. Bundercombe to call for the bill.

"I have had enough of this place!" I declared, a little abruptly. "Next time Eve goes to bed with a headache I shall take you to the club."

* * * * *

I was walking down Bond Street with Eve one morning when my suspicions as to Mr. Bundercombe and a certain matter were first roused. As we neared the Piccadilly end I distinctly saw him vanish through a doorway on the lefthand side. He was most carefully dressed and carried in his hand a long paper parcel that could contain nothing but flowers. Upon some excuse I prevailed upon Eve to cross the road. There was one small brass plate only on the side of the entrance through which Mr. Bundercombe had disappeared. It was scarcely larger than my hand and on it was engraved in very elegant characters: BLANCHE MANICURE.

I made no comment at the time, but curiously enough that afternoon, as we sat out under the trees at Ranelagh, Eve referred to the subject of her parent. "Do you notice, Paul," she asked, "how much less we see of dad lately?"

"He does seem to have been out a good deal," I admitted.

She glanced at me.

"You haven't any idea, I suppose - "

The glance and her tone were quite sufficient for me. I hastened to disclaim all responsibility for Mr. Bundercombe.

"Your father," I assured her, "has never treated me with less confidence. Whatever he may be doing at present, he is doing, let me assure you, entirely on his own responsibility."

"Then I think, if you don't mind, please," she begged, "you must try and get him to take you into his confidence. Of course," she went on, watching idly a polo team canter into the field, "I do not wish you to feel that he is in any way a responsibility. On the other hand, it does seem so queer, Paul! He has taken to dressing most carefully and he leaves the house regularly every morning at ten o'clock."

"You've no clew at all as to what he does with himself?" I asked.

"None," she replied, "except that I never saw any one with such overmanicured nails as his. I never knew him to go to a manicurist in my life, but he is obviously going to one nearly every day now or he couldn't keep the polish on. If that helps in any way - "

"It might," I admitted with a sigh.

"There he is!" Eve exclaimed suddenly. "Coming toward us, too! Do please take this opportunity, Paul, and see if you can find out anything. You see, a week ago he seemed bored to tears, and now he has just that happy, contented expression which he wears all the time when he is really engaged in something outrageous. I will go and talk to your sister. I think she is over there with Captain Green."

Mr. Bundercombe greeted me heartily and at once directed my attention to a small tent where cool drinks were being served. I suffered him to lead me in that direction and placed myself in his hands as regards the selection of a suitable beverage. We found a small table and sat down. "Haven't seen much of you lately, sir," I began.

"Huh! That's because I don't spend three parts of my time in milliners' shops," Mr. Bundercombe replied.

"Where are you spending most of your time?" I asked, determined to take the bull by the horns.

Mr. Bundercombe set down his glass.

"I've been expecting this," he remarked pleasantly. "Eve's been setting you on to pump me, eh?"

I nodded.

"That's exactly it," I admitted. "We are due to be married in ten days. We are neither of us anxious for anything in the way of an unfortunate incident."

Mr. Bundercombe appeared to view with surprise the advent of a second tumbler. He reconciled himself to its arrival, however, and handed money to the attendant.

"I realize the position entirely, my dear fellow," he assured me. "I am glad you have opened the subject up. I have been bursting to tell you all about it; but I have hesitated for fear of being misunderstood."

I glanced at his nails.

"Of course," I observed slowly, "the position of an elderly gentleman with a marriageable daughter and a wife," I went on bravely, "who finances a young lady interested in manicuring in an establishment in Bond Street is liable to misinterpretation."

Mr. Bundercombe was a little taken aback. He hid his face for a moment behind the newly arrived tumbler.

"Kind of observant, aren't you?" he remarked.

"I saw you in Bond Street this morning," I told him, "you and a paper parcel. You were entering the establishment, I believe, of Mademoiselle Blanche, whoever she is."

"Small place, London!" Mr. Bundercombe sighed. "Were you - er - alone?"

"I was with Eve," I replied; "but she did not see you and I did not mention the matter."

"My boy," Mr. Bundercombe decided, "I shall take you wholly into my confidence. I am engaged in a big affair!" My heart sank.

"I can only pray to Heaven," I said fervently, "that the dénouement of this affair will not take place within the next ten days."

"On the contrary," Mr. Bundercombe answered, leaning back in his chair and looking at me, with the flat of one hand laid on the table and the palm of the other on his left knee, "on the contrary," he repeated, "the dénouement is due to-morrow."

"Glad you didn't consider us," I observed gloomily.

Mr. Bundercombe smiled.

"I find myself in this last affair," he remarked airily, "occupying what I must confess, for me, is a somewhat peculiar position. I am on the side of the established authorities. I am in the cast-iron position of the man who falls into line with the law of the land. In other words, you behold in me, so far as regards this affair, respectability and rectitude personified. I may even choose to give our friend Mr. Cullen a leg up."

I was relieved to hear it and told him so.

"I presume," I said, "that Mademoiselle Blanche, of Bond Street, is identical with the young lady who talked to us at Stephano's the other night?"

"Say, you're becoming perfectly wonderful at the art of deduction!" my future father-in-law declared. "Same person!"

"She seems quite attractive," I admitted, "with a taste for pink roses, I think."

Mr. Bundercombe appeared to regard my remark as frivolous. He moved his chair, however, and brought it closer to mine.

"I dare say you remember," he went on, "how the young lady proposed to me that night that I should finance a little venture in which she and her sleepy-eyed friend opposite were interested."

I nodded.

"Yes, I remember that."

"From that," Mr. Bundercombe continued, "she went on to suggest that I should help her in the ambition of her life, which, it seems, was to take a single room for manicuring a few clients. In an ordinary way I should have refused that, too; and, if she had been hard up, begged to be allowed to oblige her with a trifling loan - and ended the matter in that way. The reason I didn't was simply because I felt convinced that her desire to require a single room in the manicure business was somehow associated with the scheme she had at first

E. Phillips Oppenheim

suggested. Therefore I temporized. I appeared to be interested. I asked her in what locality she wished to commence business. She never hesitated. There was only one place she wanted and that was the room she's got. Just to test her I took her to see really slap-up premises in another part of Bond Street. She pretended to look at them, but never took the slightest interest. It was just one room she wanted - and one room only.

"I realized that both she and her friend were either too desperately hard up to engage that room or else they were particularly anxious to do it in some one else's name. That was quite enough for me. I engaged the room."

I glanced once more at Mr. Bundercombe's nails. "You, at any rate," I remarked, "have been a faithful customer."

"Paul," Mr. Bundercombe continued, "I am playing a part. I am playing the part of a silly old fool. It isn't easy sometimes, but I am keeping it up. I spend a good part of my time in that beastly little parlor, having my nails done over and over again. The girl is bored to death; and I - though I flatter myself I don't show it - I guess I'm bored to death too. I've kept it up all right until now and the job comes off to-morrow. Miss Blanche is convinced that my interest in her is sentimental and she has occasionally not been quite so careful as she might have been. I have picked up here and there certain small details that enable me to form a very fair idea as to the nature of this venture in which I was invited to participate. The last few days I have been hesitating whether I should take you into my confidence or not. As it happens you have forced it. Have you anything particular to do to-morrow?"

I thought for a moment. "Nothing very much until the late afternoon, when I go down to the House," I replied.

"Then to-morrow you shall see the end of this thing with me," Mr. Bundercombe promised. "If luck goes our way you will find we shall have quite a pleasant few minutes."

Eve put her head in at the tent and we hastened to join her. She drew me a little on one side.

"I think it's all right," I told her.

"I am so glad," she replied. "And, Paul, hadn't you better drop dad a hint that Mrs. Bundercombe will be home to-morrow? I think he'd better have the shine taken off his nails!"

* * * * *

At twelve o'clock the next morning I met Mr. Bundercombe by appointment in the Burlington Arcade. We strolled slowly round into Bond Street. Mr. Bundercombe was, for him, unusually serious. He looked about him all the time with swift, careful glances. As we turned into Bond Street his pace became slower and slower. Within a yard or two of the spot where I had first seen him disappear he paused, and under pretense of talking earnestly to me he looked up and down and across the street with keen, careful glances.

At last, with a sudden turn he led the way into the passage. Together we ascended the stairs. On a door almost opposite to us at the end of the landing was another little brass plate, on which was engraved the name of Mademoiselle Blanche. Mr. Bundercombe took a latchkey from his pocket and opened the door, which he carefully closed after him.

"No one here!" I remarked.

"Not yet!" Mr. Bundercombe said, a little grimly. "From now onward you will be able to understand certain things. Miss Blanche informed me that to-day she had an invitation to go into the country. It was the only way I could discover the day in which they were planning to bring off the coup. If I had been an occasional visitor she might have risked my coming and finding her away. Since, however, I presented myself every morning at eleven o'clock she was forced to tell me. You understand as much as that?"

"Perfectly."

"You see where we are then," Mr. Bundercombe continued. "Has any reason occurred to you for the young lady's unalterable decision that no other spot in the whole of London would do for her manicure parlor?"

I looked out the window.

"We are next door to Tarteran's," I observed.

Mr. Bundercombe smiled approvingly.

"We are within a few yards," he said, "of the jeweler's shop that contains more valuable gems than any other establishment in the world. We are at the present moment within forty yards of a million pounds' worth of jewels. When you come to reflect upon the character and the past of our friend Dagger Rodwell, you will understand the significance of that fact."

I was beginning to share Mr. Bundercombe's obvious excitement. I, too, had the feeling that we were on the brink of an adventure. He made me stand up against the wall, by the side of the window, so that I could see down into the street. He himself was farther back in the room.

"Follow my lead closely in everything, Paul!" he directed. "Meantime keep your eye glued on the pavement. If things turn out as I expect there will be a gray touring motor car outside Tarteran's shop in the course of a few minutes. From that car will descend Dagger Rodwell. He will enter Tarteran's. Watch, then, as though your very life depended upon it!"

I squeezed myself against the wall and looked down upon the never-ending procession. The street was continually blocked with motor cars and taxicabs. On the other side of the way streams of people were moving all the time. I recognized many acquaintances even in those few minutes. And then suddenly I saw the gray motor car. I held out my hand to Mr. Bundercombe.

Without the slightest attempt at concealment, the man Mr. Bundercombe had called Dagger Rodwell alighted from the motor and stood for a moment looking into the windows of Tarteran's shop before he entered. He was faultlessly dressed in morning clothes, smoking a cigarette and carrying a silver-headed cane.

After some hesitation he entered the shop. Mr.

Bundercombe drew a little breath. He had been looking at another part of the street.

"Now things are beginning to move," he observed softly. "Come here, Paul!"

He pulled aside a little curtain behind which was a sort of cubicle - an easy chair, a manicurist's stool and a table.

"Step inside here," he whispered; "quickly!"

I obeyed him, and in an instant he had entered a similar one. We were scarcely there before I heard the sound of a key in the door. Through a chink in the curtain I saw Miss Blanche. She pushed back the latch and stood for a moment as though listening, her face turned toward the stairs up which she had come.

If I had had any doubt but that tragedy was afoot that morning it would have been banished by a glance at her face. She was terribly pale; her hands were shaking. Rapidly she withdrew the pins from her hat, hung it upon a peg and smoothed her hair in front of the looking-glass. Then, though her hands were trembling all the time, she filled a bowl with hot water and arranged a manicure set on a little table.

Once or twice she stopped to listen. Once, as though drawn by some fascination she was powerless to resist, she moved to the window and looked down into the street. Mr. Bundercombe remained motionless and I followed his example. At the back of my cubicle was a window from which I could still gain a view of the pavement. The streets were thronged with people, and I noticed that the motor car, which at first I had missed, was standing in a side street, almost opposite.

Suddenly I saw the man, for whose reappearance I was so earnestly waiting, step casually out on to the pavement. He attempted to cross the street and was quickly lost to sight in a tangle of vehicles. A second later I could have sworn that I saw him back again at the entrance to the passage below.

Then I heard a shout from the pavement and I distinctly saw him clamber into the motor car, which shot off as though it had started in fourth speed. An elderly gentleman, who had rushed from the shop, was halfway across the street already. There was a chorus of shouts; traffic was momentarily suspended; a policeman started running down the side street. Then I turned away from the window. There were sounds closer at hand - a footstep on the stairs, swift and gentle.

In a moment the door of the little manicure room was opened and closed. Dagger Rodwell stood there, pale and breathless. Not a word passed between him and the girl. He dashed into the third of the little cubicles, and it seemed to me that in less than thirty seconds he reappeared.

The change was marvelous. He was wearing a tweed suit and a gray Homburg hat. His eyeglass had gone. Even his collar and tie seemed different. He sat down before the girl and held out his hand. They listened. There was plenty of commotion in the street - no sound at all on the stairs.

"We've done it!" he muttered. "They're after the car! They'll catch Dolly!"

"He'll bluff it out!" she whispered.

"Sure! Don't let your hands tremble like that, you little fool! We're safe, I tell you! Get on with your work."

Now the two were three or four yards away from the cubicle in which I was, but almost within a couple of feet of Mr. Bundercombe's. From where I was sitting I saw suddenly a strange thing. I saw Mr. Bundercombe's left arm shoot out from behind the curtain. In a moment he had the man by the throat. His other hand traveled over his clothes like lightning.

It was all over almost before I could think. Rodwell was on his feet with a livid mark on his throat, and Mr. Bundercombe had stepped back with a little shining revolver in his hand which he was carefully stowing away in his pocket.

"Sorry to be a trifle hasty, Mr. Rodwell," he said. "I saw the shape of this little weapon in your pocket and it didn't seem altogether agreeable to me. We are not great at firearms over this side, you know."

Blanche and Rodwell stared at him. To complete their stupefaction I stepped out of my cubicle.

"What sort of a game is this?" Rodwell muttered, though he was pale to the lips. "Blanche - "

He turned toward her with sudden fierceness. She sat there, wringing her hands.

"Mr. Bundercombe!" she exclaimed feebly. "Mr. Bundercombe!"

"So this is your silly old fool, is it?" Rodwell hissed. "This is the old fool you could twist round your finger, who found the money for your manicure parlor, and who was in love with you, eh? What are you, anyway?" he added, turning furiously upon Mr. Bundercombe. "A cop? Is this why you were trying to put up to me a few weeks ago?"

Mr. Bundercombe waved aside the accusation.

"Nothing of the sort!" he declared.

"Then what is it you want?" Rodwell demanded. "Is it a share of the swag you're after?"

Mr. Bundercombe shook his head.

"I am afraid," he sighed, "there will not be any swag."

Rodwells face was the most vicious thing I had ever looked on; yet he kept his head. Mr. Bundercombe and I were an impossible proposition to an unarmed man.

"In the first place," Mr. Bundercombe said, "I must congratulate you most heartily on your scheme. I saw your double bolt across the road and jump into the car. Everyone's eyes were upon him. They never saw you slip round into the passage. Your double is, I presume, well supplied with an alibi and evidences of respectability?"

Rodwell nodded shortly.

"It's his own car and he's an automobile agent," he replied. "He'd been in the next shop. The people there will be able to swear to him - he gave them plenty of trouble on purpose."

"And you," Mr. Bundercombe murmured, "have the necklace?"

"I have!" Rodwell snapped. "What about it? I've got to divide with the girl here. How much do you want?"

"Only the necklace!" Mr. Bundercombe replied.

Mr. Rodwell's geographical description of where he would see Mr. Bundercombe first is too lurid for print. Mr. Bundercombe, however, only shook his head, with a gentle smile upon his lips.

"If you're not a cop and you won't stand in, what in the name of glory are you?" Rodweil spluttered at last.

"I am afraid I must describe myself as a meddler," Mr. Bundercombe confessed; "an intervener. I stand midway between the law and the criminal. I sympathize wholly with neither. I admire the skill and courage you have shown to-day, but I also sympathize with the head of that establishment whom you have relieved of possibly many thousand pounds' worth of diamonds. I could not - "

Rodwell made his effort, but Mr. Bundercombe was more than ready. Intervention on my part was quite unnecessary. Mr. Bundercombe's left arm shot out like a piston-rod and the unfortunate victim of his blow remained on the carpet, with his hand to his cheek.

"Quite in order, of course," Mr. Bundercombe remarked, "but absolutely useless. Boxing was my only sport when I was a young man, to say nothing of my remarkably athletic young companion. It won't do, Rodwell! You'd better hand over the jewels. Give them to Miss Blanche and she'll hand them to me. They're in a morocco case, I think, in your trousers pocket."

Rodwell produced them sullenly.

"It's your fault, you miserable little fool!" he muttered to Blanche. "I ought to have known better than to have let you into the thing. Fancy taking him for a mug!"

Mr. Bundercombe smiled a pleased smile.

"Come, come!" he said. "Things are not so bad. You might have been caught!"

"Aren't you going to give information?" Rodwell asked quickly.

"Not a thought of it!" Mr. Bundercombe assured him, catching the case Rodwell threw toward him. "I want, so far as possible, to see both sides happy. Here, Paul; put these in your pocket!" he added, turning to me. "If you take my advice, Rodwell," he concluded, "you'll stay where you are until I return. I promise you that Mr. Walmsley and I will return alone, and that I will give no intimation of your presence here to any person whatsoever."

Rodwell was puzzled. He rose slowly to his feet, however, and walked toward the basin at the other end of the apartment.

"All right!" he agreed sullenly. "I shall be here."

Mr. Bundercombe and I descended into the street. I

was feeling a little dazed. Mr. Bundercombe led the way into the Tarteran establishment, which was still in a state of disorder. He asked to speak to the principal, who came forward, still looking very perturbed.

"Sorry to hear of this robbery!" Mr. Bundercombe said. "Have they caught the fellow?"

"They caught the man in the motor car," the manager groaned; "but he had no jewels on him and my people can't swear to him. He seems to have a very coherent story."

"Have you communicated with the police?" Mr. Bundercombe asked.

The manager stretched out his hand.

"Four of them are in the place now," he answered, a little despairingly. "What's the good? The fellow's got away! He's got the finest necklace in the shop with him, gems worth twenty thousand pounds."

Mr. Bundercombe nodded sympathetically.

"Have you offered a reward yet?"

"We can't do everything in ten minutes!" the manager replied, a little testily. "We shall offer one, of course."

"What amount are you prepared to go to?" Mr. Bundercombe asked.

The man looked at him eagerly.

"Do you mean, sir - " he began.

Mr. Bundercombe stretched out his hands.

"You may search me!" he interrupted. "I have nothing in the way of jewels on me. My name is Joseph H. Bundercombe and I have a house in Prince's Gardens. This is my son-in-law-to-be, Mr. Walmsley, M.P. for Bedfordshire."

The manager bowed.

"I know you quite well, sir," he said, "and Mr. Walmsley, of course; both he and many of his relatives are valued clients of ours. But about the jewels?"

"What reward do you offer?"

"Five hundred pounds," was the prompt reply; "more, if necessary."

Mr. Bundercombe smiled approvingly.

"Circumstances," he explained, "of a peculiar nature, into which I am quite sure it will suit your purpose not to inquire, have enabled me to claim the reward and to restore to you the jewels."

The manager gripped him by the arm.

"Come into the office at once!" he begged.

We followed him into a little room at the back of the shop. He was trembling all over.

"No questions asked?" Mr. Bundercombe insisted.

"Not the shadow of one!" the manager agreed. "I don't

care if - pardon me, sir - if you stole them yourself! The loss of those jewels would do the firm more harm than I can explain to you."

Mr. Bundercombe turned toward me and I produced the case. The manager seized it eagerly, opened it, turned on the electric light and closed the case again with a great sigh of relief. He held out his hand.

"Mr. Bundercombe," he said, "I don't care how you got these. I have been robbed three times and put the matter into the hands of the police - and never recovered a single stone! I'd shake hands with the man who stole them so long as I got them back. How will you have the reward, sir?"

"Notes, if you can manage it," Mr. Bundercombe replied.

The manager went to his safe and counted over notes and gold to the amount of five hundred pounds, which Mr. Bundercombe buttoned up in his pockets.

"I ask you now, sir," he said, "for your word of honor that you will not have us followed or make any further inquiries into this affair."

"It is given - freely given!" the manager promised. "When you leave this establishment I shall turn my back to you. You may hand over the notes to whosoever you like upon the pavement outside and it won't concern me. Nor," he added, "shall I tell the police for at least half an hour that I have the necklace. They deserve a little extra trouble for letting the fellow get away."

Mr. Bundercombe and I left the shop and ascended the stairs leading to the manicure parlor. Rodwell, who had bathed his face and made a complete change of toilet, was pacing up and down the little room. Blanche, too, was there, still pale and weeping.

"Now," Mr. Bundercombe began, as he carefully closed the door behind him, "I told you a few minutes ago I was neither on your side nor on the side of the law. I am about to prove it. I have returned the jewels to Tarteran's, no questions to be asked, and I've got the reward. There you are, young lady!" he added, placing the roll of notes and a handful of gold in her hand. "You have given me a week or so of intense interest and amusement. There is your reward for it. If you want to divide it with your friend it's nothing to do with me. Take it and run along. So far as regards this little establishment the rent is paid for another three months; but, so far as regards my connection with it, I think I needn't explain - "

"That you've been fooling me!" the girl interrupted, a faint smile at the corners of her lips. "Do you know, sometimes I suspected that you weren't in earnest! And then one day I saw your wife - and I wasn't sure!"

"Good morning!" Mr. Bundercombe said severely. "Come along, Paul!"

CHAPTER XV

LORD PORTHONING'S LESSON

Mr. Bundercombe laid his hand compellingly on my arm. "Who's the wizened-up little insect, with a snarl on his face?" he inquired of me earnestly.

My slight impulse of irritation at such a description applied to one of my wedding guests passed when I looked up and saw the person to whom Mr. Bundercombe had directed my attention. I recognized the adequacy of the wording."

"That," I replied, "is the Earl of Porthoning."

"Kind of connection, isn't he?" Mr. Bundercombe inquired.

I nodded.

"His son married my sister."

Mr. Bundercombe regarded him with a certain wistfulness which I did not at that moment understand. Just then Lord Porthoning made his way toward us. As I watched him approach I realized more than ever the justice of Mr. Bundercombe's description. He was undersized, bent nearly double, and on his wizened face and shining out of his narrow black eyes was an indescribable expression of malevolence. Even the smile with which he greeted me had something unpleasant in it.

"Well, Paul!" he exclaimed. "Well, my boy, so you're hooked at last, are you?"

Considering that I was enjoying a few minutes' respite in my task of helping Eve receive our wedding guests, the statement, though crude, was obvious enough.

"Glad to see you, Lord Porthoning!" I said, lying miserably. "Do you know my father-in-law, Mr. Bundercombe?"

Mr. Bundercombe extended his ready hand, which my connection, however, appeared not to see.

"Yes, yes!" he admitted. "Some one pointed him out to me. I asked who on earth it could be. No offense, mind," Lord Porthoning continued; "but I hate all Americans and our connections with them. I have been looking at your presents, Paul. A poorish lot - a poorish lot! Now I was at Dick Stanley's wedding last week - married Colonel Morrison's daughter, you know. Never saw such jewelry in my life! Four necklaces; and a tiara from the Duchess of Westshire that must have been worth a cool ten thousand pounds."

"I am sorry my wedding presents do not meet with your approval," I remarked. "Personally I think it is very kind of my friends to send me anything at all."

" Rubbish , Paul! Rubbish!" my amiable connection

interjected irritably. "Don't talk like an idiot! You know they send you things because they've got to. You've been through it yourself. Must have cost you a pretty penny in your time sending out wedding presents! Now you reap the harvest."

"I suppose," I observed dryly, "that yours is the reasonable point of view."

"Absolutely, my dear fellow - absolutely!" Lord Porthoning declared. "Of course you couldn't expect quite the same enthusiasm on the part of your friends when you marry a young lady who is a stranger to all of them and who comes from the backwoods of America. Can't think how it is you young Englishmen can marry nothing, nowadays, unless it shows its legs upon the stage or has a transatlantic drawl. I am going in to see if the champagne they're opening now is any better. The first glass I had was horrid!"

My father-in-law watched him disappear through the crowd, and stood patiently by my side while I exchanged greetings with a few newly arrived friends.

"Say!" he observed presently, as soon as an opportunity rose for private conversation. "He's a pleasant old gentleman, that connection of yours!"

"Glad you think so," I answered. "I don't call myself a bad-natured fellow, and to-day I feel inclined to be friends with every one; but I tell you frankly I can't bear the sight of Lord Porthoning. He has to be asked, but he's like a wet blanket wherever he goes."

Mr. Bundercombe glanced round a moment. Then he leaned toward me. His manner was earnest -

almost pleading.

"Paul," he said, dropping his voice to a whisper, "don't you think it's up to us to give a disagreeable little worm like that a bit of a lesson, eh? His lordship has his own way too much. Now if you'll leave it to me I'll give him just a kind of a scare - a shake-up, you know - no real harm; just teach him, perhaps, not to open his mouth so much. What do you say, Paul?"

I turned and looked at my father-in-law. His expression was that of a schoolboy begging for a holiday. His head was a little on one side, his lips were parted in an insinuating smile. It was a weak moment with me. So far as such a term can be applied to such an event, the wedding ceremony, which was just over, had been a great success. Eve had looked simply as beautiful as a beautiful girl can look on the one morning of her life.

My father-in-law had been dignified and correct in his behavior, and a merciful misadventure of Mrs. Bundercombe with a policeman three days previously, which had led to her being arrested with a hammer in her satchel, had finally resulted in her being forced to partake of the hospitality of Holloway for the period of fourteen days; in fact, everything just then with me was *couleur de rose*.

The presents my crabbed connection spoke of so lightly had been supplemented only an hour before by surely the most magnificent wedding offering from my father-in-law that any man could have - the house in which we were and the whole of the furniture. It was hard to refuse Mr. Bundercombe anything. Before I knew exactly what had happened, my smile had answered his.

"Well," I said, "I rely upon your discretion, Mr. Bundercombe. A little lesson would certainly do Porthoning no harm."

Whereupon Mr. Bundercombe, fearing apparently that I might change my mind, vanished among the crowd; and the matter, to tell the truth, disappeared from my mind for a short time. I was surrounded by friends, and the occasion, joyful though it was, possessed a certain unique sentimentality that I found sufficiently absorbing. Eve brought me the latest telegram from Mrs. Bundercombe, which we read together:

Insist upon ceremony being postponed! Am commencing hunger strike. Shall be with you in three days.

"Your stepmother's intentions," I remarked to Eve, "may be excellent, but I don't think they'll bring her so far as the Austrian Tyrol."

Eve's eyes were lit with laughter. A moment later, however, she sighed.

"Poor dad!" she murmured. "I'm afraid he'll have a terrible time when she does come out!"

"He'd have a worse if she knew!" I rejoined, half to myself.

Eve looked at me suspiciously. She drew a little nearer.

"Paul," she whispered in my ear, "is it true that the inspector who had her followed all that morning was a friend of dad's?" I shook my head.

"I am giving nobody away," I replied firmly. "Of course there were certain troubles to be got over in connection with your mother's presence to-day. You remember her saying, for instance, that she would break every bottle of wine she found being served?"

Eve nodded.

"Perhaps," she murmured, with a half smile, "it is for the best. Where is dad?"

I glanced round the room and at that moment I saw Mr. Bundercombe making signs to me from the doorway. I hurried toward him and he drew me out into the hall.

"Things are in train, Paul," he announced cheerfully. "Now all I want from you is just the smallest amount of help in this little affair."

I looked at him blankly. I had forgotten all about Lord Porthoning.

"It's a very small share indeed," Mr. Bundercombe continued pleadingly; "but such as it is it's up to you to take it on at this moment. There the little insect goes into the cloakroom. He has gone for his hat and coat. All you've got to do is just to follow him and ask him to come back for one moment. That little room on the left, across the hall, is empty. Bring him into that. Leave the rest to me."

"You're not going too far, are you?" I asked. "You see, after all, the old blackguard is a sort of connection."

Mr. Bundercombe laid his hand on my shoulder.

E. Phillips Oppenheim

"My boy," he said, "there will be nothing but just a little incident that you can tell to Eve and laugh about on your way to the station. That I promise you."

I nodded and crossed the hall. Lord Porthoning was preparing to leave. "Have my car called up!" he ordered the footman from the doorstep. "Mind, I'm not going to hang about on the pavement in this sun for any one. If that's the motor waiting for the young people it'll have to get out of the way. Lord Porthoning's car at once, young fellow! Hello, Paul!" he added. "Come to see me off, eh?"

"Could I have just one word with you, Lord Porthoning?" I begged, as casually as possible.

"Be quick, then! If I haven't wished you happiness it's because I can't see what chance you have of getting it. But I suppose you're like all other young fools on their wedding day - you think the sun's shining only for you!"

"I am afraid," I retorted, a little nettled, "that I had not noticed the absence of your good wishes. I wish to speak to you on another matter."

Lord Porthoning turned quickly and looked at me. There was a change in his expression that puzzled me.

"Well, out with it!" he snapped.

I pointed to the door across the hall.

"I want you to step this way," I said firmly.

I expected an irritable outburst, but to my surprise he

turned and preceded me toward the door. We entered the room and found Mr. Bundercombe there alone. Lord Porthoning looked from one to the other of us. His heavy gray eyebrows were drawn together; his face was the embodiment of a snarl.

"Now what in the name of all that's reasonable," he began in his hard, rasping voice, "made you bring me in here? I don't want to better my acquaintance with that old man, your father-in-law! I'd a good deal rather he'd stayed in his own country. I don't like the looks of him - I hate fat men! Don't keep me waiting here, Paul. If you want my advice I'll give it to you. If you want anything else you won't get it."

Mr. Bundercombe had moved softly round until he was standing with his back to the door. His manner was the one he had assumed so successfully in church - dignified, almost solemn.

"Paul," he said, "I asked you to invite this person in here because, now that you are Eve's husband, I felt that the interests of your family must be considered before my own inclinations. In my country we treat all men alike, and I am bound to say that if you'd been married to Eve out in Okata, and I'd seen any old skunk, whether he'd been an earl or what he looks like - a secondhand clothes dealer - sneaking Eve's presents, I'd have had him in prison before you'd reached the station."

"Mr. Bundercombe!" I exclaimed, horrified; it seemed to me that my father-in-law was carrying this affair too far.

Lord Porthoning, from whom I had expected a torrent

of fierce abuse, stood looking at us both with an expression no written words could portray. His cheeks were ashen. His hands, which were crossed upon the knob of his cane, were shaking. Mr. Bundercombe extended his right hand.

"Sir," he concluded sternly, "for the sake of the conventions of the country in which I find myself, and bearing in mind your connection with my son-in-law, I have kept the police out of this interview. Be so good as to hand over to Paul the emerald brooch you have secreted in your coat pocket!"

The pall of silence seemed suddenly removed. Lord Porthoning leaned forward. Then he began to talk. Any sympathy I might have felt for him, any feeling I may have had that my father-in-law's retributive scheme was of too drastic a nature, vanished before he had finished the first three sentences. Mr. Bundercombe, upon whom he heaped abuse of the most virulent character, remained unmoved. When at last Lord Porthoning paused for breath, I turned toward my father-in-law.

"What does this mean?" I asked.

"It means," Mr. Bundercombe explained, "that this gentleman, who finds my daughter's presents so inadequate, was actually leaving your house with an emerald brooch belonging to Eve in the righthand pocket of his coat!"

Lord Porthoning was once more incoherent. This time, however, I stopped him. I was already heartily sick of the affair, but at this stage I could not back out.

"Lord Porthoning," I said, "there is no necessity for such vigorous denials. The matter is easily arranged. You had better permit me to examine the pocket in question."

"I'll see you and your common bully of a father-in-law in hell before I allow either of you to touch me or my clothing!" my pleasant connection declared fiercely. "Get out of my way, both of you! And be thankful if you don't have to answer for this outrage in a police court!"

He swaggered toward the door. Mr. Bundercombe, who had appeared to stand on one side, suddenly caught him by the shoulders.

"Feel in his right-hand pocket, Paul!" he bade me.

I did so and promptly produced the brooch. Lord Porthoning's eyes seemed almost to start from his head. I could see that he suddenly became limp in Mr. Bundercombe's grasp. His eyes were fixed on the jewels and his amazement was undeniable. Mr. Bundercombe winked at me over his head.

"What is the meaning of this, Lord Porthoning?" I demanded as sternly as I could.

My courage was failing me. I felt that the joke, after all, had been a severe one. Lord Porthoning seemed almost on the point of collapse. His eyes never once left the brooch which I was holding.

"I didn't take it!" he gasped. "I swear I didn't take it!"

I was anxious now to finish the affair.

"Lord Porthoning," I said, "I will take your word. You say you never took the brooch. Very well; we will assume, for the sake of the family, that it found its way into your pocket by accident."

Lord Porthoning felt his forehead. There were big drops of sweat standing out there. There was something in his extreme agitation that was, in a way, incomprehensible. He edged toward the door.

"I didn't take it!" he muttered. "Let me go! Let me get away!"

Mr. Bundercombe stood on one side. My hand was on the handle of the door. I looked at my father-in-law questioningly. My sympathies were now almost with the enemy, but I felt bound to see the affair through.

"It was you who discovered this little accident," I remarked. "I think you will agree with me that it is best to say nothing more about it."

Mr. Bundercombe once more winked at me solemnly over the head of my stricken connection.

"I quite agree with you, Paul," he said. "Under the circumstances we will let nothing happen to disturb the festivities and harmony of the day. Lord Porthoning certainly will not object if we just satisfy ourselves that the brooch was the only instance of - momentary aberration; shall we call it?"

If Lord Porthoning's attitude had been a little mysterious before it was absolutely incomprehensible now. He stood suddenly upright and brandished his cane over his head.

"If either of you touch me," he shouted fiercely, "I'll break your skulls! This is blackmail! I'll send for the police! Let me go!"

His sudden fit of anger, justifiable though it certainly seemed on the face of it, nevertheless took both Mr. Bundercombe and myself by surprise. The former, indeed, was in the act of opening the door, when he paused. Once more he caught my connection by the collar and thrust his hand into the other coat pocket. When he withdrew it it was filled with rings, a bracelet and a pendant.

He threw them silently - a glittering heap - on the table. Without a word he thrust his hand in once more and brought out a little black ivory carving of a Japanese monk, which was perhaps one of the most valuable of my offerings.

There was a blankness in Mr. Bundercombe's expression that I could not understand.

I frowned. It seemed to me the affair had now gone much too far. Lord Porthoning had staggered to a chair and was sitting there with his face buried in his hands. He was a stricken man. I turned to my father-in-law.

"This is too much of a good thing, sir," I whispered angrily. "The brooch was all right enough, so far as it went, and he deserved a lesson; but these other things - "

A look in Mr. Bundercombe's face suddenly froze the words upon my lips. He leaned over toward me.

" Paul," he declared earnestly , " on my honor I put

nothing into his pocket except the brooch. I knew no more of those things," he added, pointing to the table, "than you did!"

I was speechless. Lord Porthoning looked up. I had never seen a face quite like his in my life. One side of it seemed drawn with pain. He checked a sob. His fingers gripped at the air as he spoke.

"Paul," he begged hysterically, "don't give me away! I give you my word of honor - I give you my word as a Porthoning - I can't help it! You know what they call the damned thing when women have it - kleptomania, isn't it? I tell you I can't see these things without that same horrible, fascinating, cruel instinct! My hands are on them before I know it. But - " he broke off. "It's sending me mad, Paul; for, as I live, I never put hands on that brooch!"

"How long has this been going on?" I asked, almost mechanically. "Perhaps you are the reason that it has become the fashion to send detectives to guard wedding presents."

"I am the reason!" Lord Porthoning confessed, his voice shaking. "Paul, somehow I believe - I believe this has stopped it. You'll kill the instinct. Listen! You are off directly. Let this gentleman, your father-in-law, come round to my house. I will restore to him, I swear, every article I have ever taken in this fashion. He can find out the owners by degrees, and I promise that I will never again attend a wedding reception so long as I live!"

Outside I could hear them calling for me. I glanced at the clock. It was within a few minutes of the time fixed for our departure. Mr. Bundercombe nodded to me.

"Very well," I agreed. "It shall be as you say."

"I'll wait here," Lord Porthoning said in a trembling tone. "Mr. Bundercombe can come back for me after he has seen you off. He can go home with me in the motor. Take - take care of those things."

Mr. Bundercombe covered them over with an antima-cassar. We left Lord Porthoning sitting there and went out into the hall, where Eve was already waiting. Mr. Bundercombe was a little unnerved, but he pulled himself together.

"Word of honor, Paul!" he declared; "I never saw the old rat take a thing! I simply landed him with the brooch. It was not until he was going out that I caught a glimpse of those other things in his pocket."

We drove off ten minutes later. I looked out of the motor as we swung round into the main thoroughfare. Behind the window of the little sitting room I saw the pale, almost ghastly face of Lord Porthoning. He caught my eye and waved his hand weakly.

On the pavement in front of the striped awning stood Mr. Bundercombe - large, beaming, both hands outstretched. Eve waved her handkerchief. As we finally disappeared she glanced toward me.

"Has dad been up to anything, Paul?" she asked. "He has just that kind of satisfied expression that always used to terrify me."

"Like a cat licking its whiskers after a stolen saucer of

milk!" I suggested.

She laughed.

"You mustn't make fun of dad," she begged. "He's such a dear!"

"I shall never attempt to make fun of your father," I assured her fervently. "I think he is quite the most remarkable man I ever met! And now - "

www.ingramcontent.com/pod-product-compliance
Lightning Source LLC
Chambersburg PA
CBHW030118180626
46812CB00002B/465